# Also By Jerry McGahan:

*A Condor Brings the Sun* (Novel)
Sierra Club Books, San Francisco, 1996

The following stories in this collection first appeared in:
"Benediction," *The Antioch Review*, Fall 2008
"Rainy Day Ears," *The Georgia Review*, Spring 1993
"Arlene In Five," *Ploughshares*, Fall 2013
"The Deer Walking Upside Down," *The Georgia Review*, Summer 2013
"Reclamations," *The Georgia Review*, Spring 2008
"The Carolina Wren," *The Whitefish Review*, 2011
"Four Kinds of Forgetting," *The Georgia Review*, Winter 2009
"Different People's Bees," *The Montana Quarterly*, Summer 2009
"Howard's End," *The Carolina Quarterly*, Winter 2006
"Asleep In A Sturgeon," *Slush Pile*, February 2012

# The Deer Walking
# Upside Down

STORIES BY
## Jerry McGahan

schaffner
press

Schaffner Press
TUCSON, ARIZONA

First Edition
Manufactured in the United States
Cover Art: Painting by Jerry McGahan, permission granted by the Author

Cover and Interior Design by James Kiehle

ISBN: 978-1-936182-76-3 (Trade Paperback)
ISBN: 978-1-936-182-77-0 (Mobipocket)
ISBN: 978-1-936182-78-7 (EPub)
ISBN: 978-1-936182-79-4 (PDF)

# Table of Contents:

# The Deer Walking
# Upside Down

m. He can see movement at the orifice, and as his eyes adjust, forms of two or three standing on their stiltlike legs at the rance—perhaps as guards or watchmen. Watch-women. He's d about them. Only the females sting, because the stinger has veloped from the egg-laying part of their abdomen.

What now?

He starts the second to last row, at the end away from the ormer. Where will they draw the line? He listens. He can hear he television inside. War in Baghdad. This is the same month the towers fell. That image flares back, the cartoonlike fusing of building and airplane, the boil of orange, spirits lifting away like heat eddies.. He couldn't make sense of it, then or now. The bombing in Afghanistan and Iraq, all the bombing since. Is the disease of forgetting as awful as the one of remembering, of recounting?

He looks out across the valley, under pellucid blue, the fragments half gold, half green, of aspen, the buff grass and tilted lines of an old fence, everything crisp and aged and ageless, all at the same time. The glory of September. Of sixty-nine Septembers, how many could he pull apart? What does that kind of remembering mean? If the details all moosh up, there is still something large going on. An accruing like interest. Maybe it's the refining, getting the colors right, brilliant pigment on top of brilliant pigment, layers so keen, so melancholy. Here's intensity to describe old urgencies. The colors of September are out to break your heart.

"What's the matter with you, Dad?" Maureen yelled in his face, her eyes buzzing back and forth. "How could you forget that?"

"It's seized up, completely seized?" He didn't want to imagine it. Seized, it had to be.

"What happened?" She tried another tack. "Did you have it set out? The oil you were going to put in? Do you put the caps back on empty quarts? Or that's what you thought? How could you possibly forget something like that?"

# BENEDICTION

He hears the papery whir and glances about for the wasp. The colony has a nest under the eave of the shed dormer near the peak of the roof. The large golden insect hovers before his face, her dangling legs like bent spokes. The wasp's indolence seems heavy with indecision. He has the feeling she's a craft piloted by another inside. Certainly, she's stymied by his bulk, this presence blotting her path to the gray globe above. He's been an obstacle off and on now for several weeks.

Everyday he splits a row or two or three of shakes, carts them up the ladder, and nails them down. Jimmy Lord can still make a good cedar shake, even though he won't claim the classic design. There's no taper. They come out almost thick as a deck of cards their entire length, because he doesn't flip the bolt every time he splits one out. It's true he's using twice the wood he needs for the job, which is the same as saying he's wasting half. When he tore off the old shakes, the ones he'd made twenty-four years ago, the thin, splintery, dust and lichen-laden lower halves, gray and crumbly, attached to covered wood that was smoked-salmon orange, thick and fresh as the day he nailed them down. So a thin tapered end would serve as well covered by the bottom half of the shake above. Wasted wood or no, Jimmy persists, mostly because he likes the lovely fluting of consistent thickness that develops at the bottom end.

His neighbors are all going to steel roofing. Won't be roofing that one again, they say. Even with these comparatively short-lived shakes, it's safe to say that Jimmy Lord won't likely be doing this roof again either. And next summer, he'll re-roof the chicken house—if he can get any of the firewood sawyers to find him some cedar bolts.

He likes splitting shakes. There's something about the sound of tearing wood, that stretching pull before the report, and the shake flying like a shot off a shovel. The smell, too, faint but aromatic, the fresh insides of a fine tree. Two or three rains and the color of the roof fades, but the keen lines and clean texture of this old-time craft sure beat the hell out of enameled steel.

Sucking in a breath, he forgets the hovering wasp, frets instead about Maureen, the expression she had when Roberta brought her back. All that anger streaming out like yellow jackets. He'd always changed the oil for her. He can remember her first car, the beat-up Escort in high school, then the Hyundai in college, he can remember that, and the Buick when she got married, then the Subaru wagon, the Volvo, the Toyota when she was divorced. He can remember their colors. So how does he remember all that but forget to put the oil back in her Bronco? There are telegraph lines inside him that have gone down.

He picks up a shake and examines its light toughness. When he shook his first building, the wellhouse, a quarter century before, he did it with larch instead of cedar because he'd gotten a deal on a big larch log. Even if larch didn't split as easily and perfectly as cedar, he reckoned to make up for that with his own tenacity. Or as Roberta would have it, bullheadedness. He made the long chisel blade from a truck spring. He fitted the wrap-around end with a juniper handle. The first malls he chopped from alder and cotton-

wood, and then tired of busting them into p[...] an ugly but serviceable alternate cobbled out [...] a carved handle with a block nailed on either [...] replacement blocks he slapped on as they split or [...]

When he bought the larch he knew to get a log [...] but he didn't know to watch for twisted grain. That i[...] plied him with a whole tree of two-foot propellers. [...] ever, he used them anyway. Jimmy stood on each pai[...] diagonal corners and beat in a handful of six-penny [...] Pounds of nails later, the roof still came out looking li[...] potholders in a northwest gale, or as if someone had cri[...] the bottom left corner of every shake to get a peek beneat[...]

Rueful, he glances at the eave where the wasps thrive[...] put up with them one day too many. Today he reaches the[...] Since beginning, he's planned on destroying their paper h[...] But there it hangs, shaped like a plump tornado, a Chinese l[...] tern loaded with sparks. He thought to tear it loose with a pol[...] at dawn when it was cool, and then spray them down with th[...] hose, chill them thoroughly, push the paper pulp and the clot of [...] drenched insects down the roof and over the eave into the ca-lendulas where he could finish them off handily with more water. Trouble was, trouble is, he never got around to it, mostly because of the restraint they'd shown him. He'd been waiting for that first sting, solid provocation. Everyday he got that much closer, his expectancy for attack mounting, either by those angered with his hammering, or simply in reaction after bumping into him, which they've done daily. But it hasn't happened. Not one sting. He'd even brushed one from his neck.

The one hovering before him tips slightly like a helicopter and motors away, dips, and disappears under the dormer eave. He stoops, peers up into the constriction where the nest hangs, gray marbled paper gently ribbed like the settling weight of soft ice

Possibly? He didn't know. Maybe the cap thing. He did replace them, as a habit. On the empty quarts. He couldn't remember finishing. A glop of time had slipped away from him, a hole in his pocket.

Her face scared him. She wanted to hunt him down, capture him. He puts a nail in his mouth. Like the president says he's going to hunt down the terrorists. Jimmy glances at the eave. He doesn't want to get stung on the lip or ear or eyelid, some place like that.

"You're not listening to me," Roberta said.

"I am. I always listen to you." They were eating breakfast. He thrust his head. She never talked to him like this, not with that kind of thin-lipped accusation. Besides it was true, he always listened to her.

"I told you she wanted us to come tonight for Lindy's birthday. She's working Friday and won't have time to get ready for it." Lindy is Maureen's eight-year old daughter.

"That's fine. That's fine." He showed her his hands. No weapons. "I don't have other plans if that's what you mean."

"Jimmy, I told you last week, I told you yesterday."

"You're balancing the checkbook now, too, because my math's gotten a little rusty. Same thing."

"No, Jimmy. It's not the same thing."

He rubbed his forehead furiously. "It just isn't sticking like it used to, that's all."

She watched him with working eyes.

He smiled reassurance.

But she was having none of it.

He's up to the eave. One, two, three rows below the nest. He puts two nails in his mouth, lengthens himself, stretching up to extend the shake that edges the dormer. He sets the first nail, then takes four blows to drive it in. Two wasps emerge, stand on the lip upside down, watching. When he drives in the second nail, another wasp joins the first two. He gets the shake nailed down before they do anything. A little wobbly, he draws back and trundles on all threes across the roof to start the next to the last row. If he had to, he could wait for that last little area, wait till after the snow flies. Except he wouldn't do that, wouldn't climb up on an icy roof, wouldn't wait either. Something about finishing a job. He'd probably forget, for Christ's sake.

Those two women in his life, two fires he had to keep after. But it's this latest turn that's got him scared the most. They've quit harping. In fact, they were treating him like a king. Or a child. Last week, Maureen came up behind him when he was at the kitchen table trying to get a full Nelson on the crossword puzzle. She gripped his shoulders, then bent over, wrapped her arms around his neck, clung like she was pulling him from the maelstrom.

"Hey," he gasped, "what's this?" But she wouldn't say anything, wouldn't let him see her face. It might've been nice enough all right, but it left him feeling like that kid again, a new kid, the one standing over by the swing-set getting talked about and pointed at.

Suddenly, it seems, he's back to the eave of the dormer, eleven inches closer to the nest on this row. Stretching, he fits the shake to size, then backs away and sets the two nails. He's disturbed at his intention, this kind of inside subterfuge moving like a glacier.

The nest is quiet, until he hits the first nail. A knot of wasps—he isn't counting anymore—congregates at the mouth of the nest. He does not pause. He does not hurry. It's like he's in a car or a diving plane, and the steering is stuck, and there's nothing he can do but ride it out. He's sweating-wet, but the terror gathering is no longer that he will be stung, but that he will not, that they will allow him, make him try for the last row, and that's a picture he doesn't like at all. To reach that last shake properly, he'll have to curl up under the eave, fist, face, and torso stuffed in the same small space with the nest, his hammer flying.

For reasons he cannot comprehend, they don't sting him. Although he's slippery wet, droplets jerking down his sides, he stands away surveying, feeling like cold water has been diverted into his veins. There's somebody inside getting ready. The last row takes a shorter shake. He measures, descends the ladder, handsaws what he needs for the final row, and then trundling them in his sling, mounts the roof again.

He can hear the television. Intermittently. Three days past, and they're still showing it. He tries to imagine jumping from seventy stories up. He'd have to be in a helluva state to take the leap. Fire or mindless fear, maybe. Or maybe just mindless would be enough.

No. Not that one. With mindless, there's a catch. Too mindless to go on living amounts to the same as too mindless to jump. That's the snag that fills nursing homes.

"You look good, Dad," Maureen says every day now, "real good." But her face is crooked, thwarted.

Three shakes from the nest, the alerted wasps have gathered outside, a bramble of weaponry. Any one-sting warning is out the window now. He nails in the first of the last three shakes, fits the second, and sets the nails. Driving them in, he can hear the wasps bristle at each blow, but none arrows out at him.

Must be a hundred degrees up here, he guesses. He takes off his straw hat so as to get himself under the eave. Sweat trickles into one eye. He blinks. He guesses at the width of the last shake and sets the nails. Then he slithers up under the eave, keeping the colony in an unfocused haze as he devises where the lever of his muscles and bones must go to understand the nail, where his flesh will not bump that deadly haze, to manage all of this in such a way as to broadcast his single intention. He ends up with his face, his neck, shoulder, and arm curled round the pendant colony. Just as he'd pictured it, impossible as it seems. In your face. And mine. Brightly colored oragami, crisp and brittle and rattly pissed.

He lifts his hammer for the first blow but there's no space for drawing back. The claws hit the eave. Ah. He swallows. Have to batter these nails in. He rotates the hammer so as to strike the nail with the side of the head. How perfectly inefficient. Astonishingly awkward. He lifts and smacks the nail. The wasps flare.

Jimmy Lord blinks. Sweat runs in a sheet, and he can't see well. Still, there's no cascade of embers spilling over him. He begins the beating, and through the burning blur watches the choreography of their pulsing, bristling accompaniment. In some sidelong pocket of time, he drives the first nail, and without faltering, moves to the second, and drives it in.

He hesitates some part of a second, blindly suffused with incredulity and a magnificent stillness, of a sort that follows a prayer. Unaccountably placid, he unfolds himself from around their contained violence, withdraws, and restored to that other infinite setting, stands fresh again in September. He wipes for a time at his eyes. He bows slightly at them. Then he finds his hat and puts it on, gathers his sling and the extra shakes, his can of nails, his hammer, and edges stiffly down the roof. Watching his feet, he descends the ladder. A swatch of lawn beneath, so very beautiful somehow, all green and cool and complicated, ratchets itself toward him.

# RAINY DAY EARS

She is standing on my porch; I'm in my doorway. It's all I can do to hear what she's saying—something about a dog—not because of how or what she says, but because of who she is: Sara Carling. Easy enough to say, a name, a woman, except that she's a secret I've kept for thirty years. She's what I think about when I'm not thinking of anything in particular. I think about her everyday, so if we're doing grains of sand, I've got my own Sara-Carling beach.

So, there she is, standing there like just anybody—on my porch—and I'm doing the best I can to look natural and working like hell to keep up with what she's saying. I look at her face. I watch her eyes, the lines down her nose, the lips, the white ends of her teeth, a loop of hair in front of one ear.

I am Bert Ritter, government trapper, bachelor, gardener. Pretty soon I'll be fifty.

Once she was Sara Carling. Is. I avoid her married name. Actually I don't even know it, or if she still has it. Sara Carling, two words I carry like my own ears and nose. Ten years ago I visited a cousin in Minnesota to do some pike fishing, and one evening I fell asleep in front of the TV. When I woke up, Mort's wife asked me who Sara Carling was. I didn't ask what I'd said.

I don't consider myself a coward. There's nothing in the hills that scares me—scares me so I dread it, I mean. Plenty that lives there has my respect, but that goes for mice as well as bears. Which is to say it's hard to surprise me. But as I stand there in my doorway not five feet from Sara Carling, it's all I can do to keep from seizing up.

"...gitters on Walt Carney's place, so I called him..." she says.

A gitter is a rawhide-wrapped housing for a pistol cartridge loaded with cyanide powder. It's about the size of a shot glass, and it's fastened along with a firing pin assembly to a short length of pipe pounded into the ground. I use gitters to kill coyotes.

She's wearing denim pants, faded, that thin denim women wear, and an orange sweatshirt with a white shirt underneath. The starched collar is showing. Her eyes are blue and her gaze direct and unswerving as a courthouse clerk's. I hear the question coming and start grabbing at the words, so I can answer. She's lost her dog. Do I have gitters set out nearby? "Where are they on Walt's place?" she asks.

Answering, my voice sounds funny, like a recording. She describes where she lives, and this gives me time to get a hold on myself and look at her, too. It's pretty funny, her directions, that is. I know the outside of her house better than the inside of my own. I hear her climbing toward another question.

"...must be two miles or so. Could he have gotten to those gitters?"

"If he went the two miles. Is he cut?"

"Yes."

"Does he run, wander I mean?"

"He hasn't before," she says, pinning me with those eyes. I try to keep from looking at the white line of her teeth, the wetness inside her mouth. The tiny lines at her mouth and the corners of her eyes look like wear marks on buckskin.

"A gitter would kill him," she says. This one she tries to make a question, wants it only a question.

"Yes," I tell her.

Thirty years ago when I was a greenhorn trapper, I was scooting down Rat Creek Road in my jeep, smacking puddles and skating across the grease and leather of half-dried gumbo. Wahooo! Rounding one corner, I came onto a '52 Ford stuck in a big hole. I didn't know her name then. She was only eighteen and had just graduated that spring.

I hooked up my winch and went to work. I'd never seen beauty like that before. It was all I could do to manage the job. I got clumsier and muddier and more pathetic at every turn. I did keep my distance. I hadn't shaved for a few days, and I smelled bad—the stink of sweat was the least of it, given the rotten meat I used for bait scent. I tipped my cap and got out of there.

Sometimes I think I might've been a happier man had that day never happened. Maybe I never would have ever seen her close enough, seen the way her eyes were calm and even and smooth looking into mine, seen that skin and those teeth, heard that voice. Of course, that happiness or just plain peace I didn't get was worth as much as the haunting she's done me. I can go a long time just knowing I have a chance to glimpse her again.

She lives along the highway at Upside Corner. Upside Corner is on the way to everywhere for me. Sara's house is a small white house with green trim. She has a large front lawn with too many lilacs—too many places to hide her. After high school, she spent summers out at her folks' place on Rat Creek, and I never saw her except once a year or so at rodeos or street dances, where I kept a respectful distance. She went away to college those years, so I had a modicum of peace in the winters, except for Christmas break, when I went downtown every day and watched the streets. In four Christmases I only saw her once, coming out of Ben Franklin's with an armload of packages. She walked tall and straight and easy. She was wearing a man's Mackinaw and men's overshoes, unbuckled. I've never gotten over how womanly she was in the clothes of a man.

From the newspaper I learned when she graduated from college. That same year she got married. And I was glad of it. I figured I could go from there, that it was like when I quit Copenhagen. Thinking about tobacco, about quitting chew, was twice as bad as doing it. One day I just wiped it out of my brain, and that was that. But not Sara. There was that woman's figure and the woman's way of walking dressed in men's winter clothes, and the lines of that face, winter ivory, and she walked back and forth, in and out of my head. She didn't live in Armstead anymore. I didn't know what her husband did or where they lived or what her name was. But I couldn't quit her like I quit chew.

She was gone for twelve years. Then, one day there she was at Upside Corner. I was going out to the Frying Pan—a big prairie flat, a basin that cooks in the sun—and there was Sara Carling standing at the mailbox looking through her mail. Her hair was blowing across her face, and she pulled it back with one hand, did it without lifting her eyes from the envelopes she was sorting. I could see she was thinner and older, but—goddamnit—it had all been to her favor. Like weathered wood: sun-cured but out of the rain, where the knots turn deeper, richer gold against the iodine of the smooth grain. Her skin was darker, yet it seemed half translucent. I whisked by in my jeep. I was shaking, and I could hear funny little catches in my breathing. That was thirteen years ago.

I don't know what happened to her marriage, but she came back alone. She bought the place on Upside Corner and got a job as a clerk in Penney's. I haven't been in there since. In the winter, I saw her wading through the snow to her mailbox, her big black-and-brown dog following. In the summer, I could see her sometimes mowing the lawn—catch a piece of her before she went behind a lilac or just coming out. Usually I saw her coming out or going back from the mailbox. I always happened to be driving by Upside Corner right after the mail had been delivered.

I collected pictures of her—recollections just like pictures—in the same way kids collect baseball cards. Here's one: Sara Carling pruning a lilac. She stands on a stool, stretches upward on her toes, her arms reaching above with pruning shears. She is wearing cutoffs. Her legs are lean, exactly alike, with sharp lines from the muscles working to stretch. Her cutoffs are not tight but they follow her right, tattletale cutoffs to make her naked in the same way a smile can make a face seem naked. Her back is straight and narrowing to her waist, partly hidden by a wild mane of hair. She has strong shoulders and forearms.

Another: she's reading a letter. That's all. The sound of my passing, the noise and blot of it, means nothing. I stare at the profile of her face, the lines of her nose and lips, the fluting beneath her nostrils, the tip of her tongue, the cords in her neck, the large, quiet, letter-listening eyes.

A third: she must have slipped on the ice. She was standing, half-bent whisking snow off her butt. Mouth open, she was laughing aloud. I imagined the sound, hard and forceful, bright as the smell of just cut juniper. I found myself laughing, heard my own sound join what I pretended to hear of hers.

Having Sara Carling on my porch, asking, talking, seeing me see her, is not something I could have prepared for. The two of us watch to see what I will do: she, with the average expectation of one human speaking to another, while I'll have to tell a kind of lie. Bert Ritter and Sara Carling will have this conversation, and it will be like any two people standing on a porch, one saying something the other understands, the other answering, all of it with a plain pig-in-the-mud-sense.

"Walt doesn't know exactly where they are. Will you tell me so I can go see? My dog has never been gone overnight." Her voice has a lot in it, more sound per square inch, a sound like vanilla smells. Distilled.

"There isn't any road to them, and there aren't any landmarks in that flat, out there in the Frying Pan. But I can take you out."

"Will you? When?"

"Right now?"

"I'd appreciate it."

"We'll take my jeep." I point to it in the driveway. "Let me get a gun and my field glasses." I go back into the house. On the way back out I look through the window just to make sure she hasn't dissolved.

There she is, sitting in my jeep. I can see the only way I'm going to get through this deal is by not believing it. A pipe dream. I take a breath and step out the door. I drive us out of town. We go by Upside Corner. Together—she out loud, and I mouthing it to myself—we say, "That's where I live."

The dog now, I am thinking; she will tell me about the dog.

"His name is Brando," she says. "His mother was a Newfoundland—"

"And his father, ten of the finest dogs in town?"

She smiles, but does not look at me. I frown at my wise-ass remark.

The gitters are only two miles from Upside Corner but we have to take a road to the Frying Pan that circles in from the north, a road that adds another eight miles or so. The last gate is locked, but I have the key Walt gave me. I turn off the jeep, unlock and open the gate, close it again. When I get in, she asks, "Do you have to lock up property with gitters on it?"

"No." It finally occurs to me that she probably resents me. I may not be the reason her dog is missing, but the possibility is enough. Maybe she'll hate me, and I'll find some way of getting shed of her, of not thinking about her every day.

"Gitters are different than the poison?" she asks.

"Poison?"

"Don't you poison coyotes?"

"Ten-eighty, you mean?"

"Is that what it's called?" Maybe there's a little snippiness in her voice.

I glance at her. She's lived in my head so long that seeing her sitting there looking straight ahead is like being drunk for the first time. I've got nothing to compare it to. "Ten-eighty. It's a poison, but I don't use it anymore. I wouldn't use it this near to town anyway."

"What's not poison about a gitter? There's a poison inside." She's looking for my throat. A big old bear of sadness crawls up under my chest and fixes to bed down. Winter's coming.

Even so, I've got nothing but the truth for her. Who could lie to someone they've ached over for thirty years? What she doesn't like about me isn't going to steal anything I've never had. I suppose I could stay fool enough for her anyway, so that whether she likes me or not won't matter. Except…way down at the bottom of me, it seems that if I like her that much and she can't persuade me out of it, then somewhere down deep in her there has to be a part of her that is me, something she can do nothing about. Sounds like a misty bleeding hope, but there are some things I know even when I don't know how I know. She'll never know she carries a government trapper around, a little chunk of one anyway. That's how I look at it.

"When I used ten-eighty, I took a horse to a high ridge, a pass over five or six thousand feet high and at least ten miles from any house. Shot it and injected it with ten-eighty. I did it in the fall, and then in late spring I went back for what was left. What I cleaned up I threw down a mine test-shaft. A gitter has cyanide in it—a poison, that's right—but it's packed in a pistol cartridge. It gets one coyote, each gitter does. That's all. It's not the same as a whole horse filled with poison, where a coyote eats a load, vomits it somewhere else, and dies, but kills any other coyote that eats what that one threw up. It's a different kind of deal altogether."

She doesn't say anything. I take a look. Her face is hard. "Nasty business, either way, I guess. You guess, I mean."

"Yes," she says.

"So what will you do, Sara, if I've killed your dog?"

"I will cry." She looks at me. "How did you know my name?"

"I think you told me. My name is Bert Ritter."

I can feel her staring. It bumps at the side of my face. She is alert, disturbed. It comes over me like a scent.

"There's a coyote," I tell her. I can see it a half mile away. A yellow gold blot not eighty yards from the gitters and the dead sheep I used for bait. "A dead one." She follows my eyes but doesn't seem to see it until we're almost there. I stop the jeep with the coyote alongside my door, but she leaps out and runs around the vehicle to look at the animal. It's been dead a day or two. It looks like it's still running, except that it's on its side, legs stretched out in a scared, stopped lope. "I have to take the ears," I tell her. I take out my jackknife, kneel, and do the job. I can't tell if it's a sound she makes, or it's just her breathing, but I know what she's thinking. She's imagining me doing something like that to her dog. I flip the scalp into the back of the jeep.

"That's all you take?" she asks. "Just the ears?"

"That's it. I skin them in the fall before they start rubbing, but the hide's not worth anything now. Besides, out here in the sun the hair's slipped."

"What do you do with ears?"

"Fry 'em in bacon grease."

She's not amused.

"No. My supervisor takes what I got when he comes through. They're like ticket stubs for a highway patrolman. That's how they keep tabs on my work."

I don't tell that her that he won't be seeing these ears for a while. I have an extra bag of ears salted away. Rainy-day ears, a month's worth of work—the measure for it, anyway—in case I get laid up or something. I circulate every set of ears through that bag so none of them gets to looking too old.

Sara kneels and touches the coyote's side, pets it. The animal doesn't smell too good. I look at its earlessness, the strip of red across the top of its skull. I look at it to see what she sees. It's not so pretty. A person can forget what something looks like.

"So where are the gitters? How do we know about Brando?" She's looking up at me from where she's kneeling, and I get caught again on that merry-go-round of not believing. I'm standing here, and she's kneeling there on the same card-table-sized piece of ground, and she's speaking to me.

I was afraid to look at these gitters, but if the dog had gotten into them, we'd have found him by now. He wouldn't run far if he got shot, and there's no place to hide.

Sara follows me to the sheep. More than likely, it was the dead coyote that killed this sheep I used for bait. I start to tell her that, but squeeze it off. It might sound like an excuse. I examine the three gitters. Only one has been fired. I show her the fired one. I pull the pipe out of the ground and show her the catch that hooks to the firing pin assembly. "It's just a little barrel, no longer than the cyanide cartridge, and it's wrapped in rawhide and painted with scent." I pull out the fired cartridge and slide in a new one, and then I thread the little cylinder back into position on the pipe stake. "See, the coyote sniffs it, bites it, and then when he pulls on it, the cartridge goes off and shoots the cyanide down his throat."

She looks nauseated. "This is the one that got that coyote?"

She glances over her shoulder.

"Yes."

"And that's the only one fired."

"That's right."

"Would you...would you consider unhooking these until I find my dog? I know you have no reason to do that, but I . . ."

"Sure," I say, "sure I would." Stooping to unthread them, I keep my face turned where she can't see it, can't see the pleasure I'm taking. I guess there's nothing that I've ever wanted more than to have another chance like this, and I'm willing to do it no matter how it looks, even if it is the not-so-pretty request that I don't kill her dog. I'm glad these gitters didn't get her dog, and I'm happy as a kid to pull them.

"I never told you my name," she says.

"I got shot once with a gitter. Shot my hand," I tell her.

"Did it kill you?"

Didn't do a thing. I had on cotton gloves, like these. Turned my palm yellow, that's all. Had me sweating for a minute, though."

"Thought you were a coyote?"

"I've always been a coyote. It takes one to catch one."

This time I see her smile. I know that I will always tell her the truth. I will do that for me, for what I love. But knowing this puts a cold hand around my heart. The questions I don't want to her to ask. What else do you do to get these coyotes? She could ask that.

I use poison, traps; I call them in with a predator call, then shoot them. I could tell her that I find the dens and rock up the entrances so the bitch can't get to the litter. Then I leave the pups for a week, starved enough so that they're either dead or pretty limp. I pull out all the rocks, and there they are, pressed up at the top where they've tried to get out, tried to get to the bitch. Any that are still whimpering I rap on the head. The day before yesterday I got five sets of ears. Little ears. The government doesn't dock anything for size. One coyote is one coyote. If she ever asked me, I'd tell her. As it is, I'll see no more of her than I ever have. Doesn't matter. I won't lie to her.

Then a funny thing happens. It puts a kink into what I've settled on being for her. We're bouncing along out of the Frying Pan, nobody saying anything until I see this ledge of sandstone running out along the pan's handle. I point to it. "There's some little cactus in bloom on that ledge. They're not prickly pear. A little barrel cactus, sort of—don't run across them very often—with pink flowers. Would you like to see them?"

I didn't know I was going to ask her that. Sometimes, I just watch myself, like I'm somebody else, just to see what happens. It's a pleasant little exercise, and lately, it's gotten to be more of a habit, enough so that I just slip into it when I'm not looking. This is a bad time not to be looking.

She doesn't answer at once, and I realize this could-have-been killer of her dog is getting another chance. What the hell? I think, rising out of myself, the day isn't over yet. "And there's a pretty Indian Paintbrush just over the rise, a kind of fluorescent pink one that just grows out here on the flats when the spring is wet."

"Okay." That's all she says.

We climb the ledge and find a half dozen or so of the stubby little cactuses. They look like the end of one of those cactuses you can buy in Safeway at times, one that's mostly buried and can't quite break out of the ground. One cactus has four blossoms. Cautiously, she kneels and puts her nose to the flowers. "No smell," I laugh, "just pretty." It's really something to see her face bent down over those little flowers. If she were my wife or girl friend, even my sister, I'd have to say something about how they make each other look so nice. Behind her, the Frying Pan is heating up and the warbly little heat waves make everything squirm. The sky is so goddamn blue I want to holler. I don't hurry her. We just kind of wander around, and the words we don't say are as fine as anything could be.

By and by, she looks at me, and I know she is ready to see the paintbrush. We mosey down the hill on the backside of the ledge and I show her some Draba. These are tiny little plants with tight little grayish leaves like juniper needles and a bright crown of gold flowers. They're earlier than the cactus so I have to poke around for awhile to find one under the shade of a sage that's still in good color.

She makes a sound when she sees the paintbrush. A little sound. All order of things happen inside me to hear it. There I am finding out that of all the wool gathering I have ever done about Sara Carling, I missed dreaming the thing I wanted to do with her the most.

I tell her that most paintbrush lives in the mountains, the orange and red and creamy yellow ones, and that it is a plant which does funny little things with its roots, borrows as much as it makes, from what or where nobody knows, that they are like mushrooms and flowers both so that they don't care to be transplanted. I tell her it's one that I've never tried to put in my garden, that I just have to wait for wet springs and go to the Frying Pan, which has been just as well anyway. Everything I say she seems to understand. All of it, I mean.

By and by, we're back to the jeep and I drive her back to town, back to my house and her car. We get out of the jeep and she thanks me for taking her out to the gitters and for pulling them, and then she thanks me for showing her the flowers. Of course, I say.

She goes to her car, and I go in the house. But I come back out when she drives away, and I watch her car go down the street. I'm still taking everything I can get.

# Arlene In Five

# 1.

When the brindled cow was five, she got an infected eye. Arlene took her to the vet in Armstead to have the eye examined, perhaps removed. The brindled cow wasn't worth the vet bill, but she was a pet of sorts. Arlene loaded the cow into the horse trailer, delivered her to the vet's holding pen in back, gave her some hay and water, then unhooked the trailer and left to pick up supplies. When she returned several hours later, the vet had cut out some tissue surrounding the eye and shot her up with antibiotics, a wait-and-see measure. On the way out of town, Arlene remembered the wiring and receptacles Leonard wanted for a renovation project on part of the hay barn. She parked in the lot behind the hardware store and went in the back door. She returned to find the trailer door open and the cow gone.

Haltingly, Arlene circled the truck; she found herself holding the bag of wire and receptacles out in front of her as if offering them to someone, a trade for her cow. She got in the truck, drove around the shopping center, then circled several of the adjoining blocks. She went back to the center and called the police. "Yes," the dispatcher said. "She's on her way down Holcomb right now, and she's got a crowd on her heels. You better get down there. Last

I heard she was in the eight-hundred block."

"Tell them not to chase her."

"I can't get him on the radio. Go find them."

Arlene hung up and ran to the truck.

Arlene found scattered flops of manure in the seven-hundred block, but she saw nothing on ahead. She turned right. The trailer clattered behind. She slowed, found nothing east, crossed Holcomb heading west then and found them two streets across. The cow had collapsed on someone's lawn. Her tongue was out, her head sagging onto the ground. Several dozen children, some on bikes, clumped before her. Adults in twos and threes stood farther back out on the sidewalk and in the street where the police car, lights flashing, had lodged itself at an angle against the curb. It was like a parade, something festive. Arlene left her truck in the middle of the street and ran. "Leave her be!" she yelled.

An elderly couple stood on their porch looking down at the stricken animal. The old man had a newspaper in his hand. She had on her apron. "What?" the policeman said. He was standing nearest the cow, his hands propped on his hips.

"Why did you chase her?" Arlene cried. "Look at her." She dropped to her knees alongside the stressed animal and caressed the big, sagging head. The cow's breathing was shallow and rapid.

"She was loose. How we supposed to catch her?"

"Not by chasing her," Arlene barked. She hears the hush, the change of mood like a cloud over the sun. "If you would've left her alone, she would've stopped. Look at her now."

"She was running. You don't make her stop by watching her run away. She could cause wrecks, damage people's yards. You're the one at fault here, letting her out."

"I didn't let her out. Who did this?" She glanced around. When several boys backed away a little, she glared at them.

"We didn't do anything," one said.

"I've got to get her back to the vet," she told the policeman. "Can you help me load her?"

"Of course. Look—"

But Arlene wasn't listening. She ran back to the truck. First, she angled the vehicle's nose across the street and into a driveway. Cranking first one way, then another, she backed the trailer up to the curb behind the police car, gunned the engine, and popped the trailer wheels up onto the boulevard. A few limbs cracked overhead when the top of the trailer pushed through the lower canopy of a tree. The policeman's arms flew out but she did not slow, backed the trailer directly to the cow. She got a rope from behind the seat. The policeman was saying something to the old couple on the porch. The brindled cow looked worse, all flopped out, her sides heaving. Arlene dragged out the little ramp from beneath the trailer, butted the back end under the cow's neck, then tied the rope around her neck. She gave the rope to the policeman, who was stooping over, watching. "You pull from inside the trailer. Let up when I tell you to let her breathe. Can I get help from anybody else to push her?" she called out. A small crowd, maybe eight or nine men and several women, drew forward. "Behind and alongside," Arlene directed, "just push her up this ramp." The cow could not stand. Grunting, most of them on their knees squeezed in alongside each other, their hands lined along the cow's backside, some hands atop others, pushed. The cow slid up the ramp and into the trailer. Arlene leaped out, waited for the policeman to exit, then slammed and latched the trailer door.

"Is she sick?" the policeman asked. "I mean, was she?"

"I got to get her back." She pointed off across the city, then hopped into the cab. She edged the trailer over the curb, and then accelerating evenly, sped away. But by the time she got to the veterinarian's, the brindled cow was dead, her tongue draped out, her legs kicked out straight.

"Why? Why would they do that?" she asked Leonard that night. They were sitting at the kitchen table. "Why would they chase her to death?"

"They didn't know, Arlene."

"I don't get it." Arlene couldn't stop shaking her head. "That poor old cow, that sweet, sweet animal. They just ran her to death. They didn't stop till she was done for."

"What do they know about cows? Just like kids from town when they come out here always wanting to chase the chickens."

"They had no sense. None of them. That policeman, he ought to know something about suffering animals. I don't know how you can defend any of them."

"Because I don't think they would've chased her if they knew it'd kill her."

"You can't say that, Leonard. You should of seen them lined up around her, watching her die. They weren't afraid for their lawns or gardens, or somebody crashing into her. They wanted some action. Like she was a sacrifice or something."

"Get a grip, Arlene. You got a right to be mad, but don't lose sight of yourself."

"I want to lose sight of myself. I lost the brindled cow today, and they all thought it was great fun."

"Well, you're going to have to get over it."

"I don't want to get over it."

"I know. Stew in your juices then. See where that gets you."

"Don't you do that smug thing to me."

"It wasn't me that killed your cow, Arlene. I'm going to shut my mouth now, till it's safe again."

"I hate that smug thing you do."

But Leonard wouldn't be badgered back into the ring. Arlene went out and stood on the back porch, let the cool night wind blow on her fire. The sky shimmered with bits of icy light. Take the arc to Arcturus, she said, drive the goddamn spike to Spica.

# 2.

"You going through something, Arlene?"

"Sit down. Get undressed."

He shook his head, watched her. "All the way naked?" His expression was something between astonished and apprehensive. "That couch isn't big enough for the both of us, Arlene. It's the middle of the goddamn day."

"It was big enough for us thirty years ago. So what if it is the middle of the day?"

"What is this? Something you been reading in those magazines?"

She stopped unzipping her pants. "What's the matter, Leonard? You're not interested anymore?"

His expression is quizzical.

"Don't you remember when it didn't matter? Remember in the hammock? The back of the pickup?"

"That's a long damn time ago, Arlene." But he was undoing his belt and watching her.

She slipped off her bra and then went back to her pants. So what if it was a long time ago? "Here, let me help you, Leonard."

"Get away. God, you're nuts." He turned, chortled.

"No."

"Goddamn it. Arlene, quit that. Arlene. Arlene..." he trailed off.

A few days later, he came in early for lunch. He sat on the couch, made half a wink, and wagged his head once, a "come-on-over-here" wag. She told him the couch was too small, and it was the middle of the day. And then four months after that, there they were sitting in Doctor Snelling's new-carpet-smelling office getting told about Leonard's pancreas, and three months later Leonard Darr was gone. Just gone. He wasn't out in the barn. She could look out the window, and there was the truck, but he wasn't there, not out in the corrals, not in the house, not in the bathroom, not on the back porch looking for the mate to his glove, not in the refrigerator drinking from the orange juice pitcher. Nowhere.

# 3.

It was somewhere in between the knowing and the dying when her father-in-law came to see her. She heard his car approach and looked back over her shoulder to see him getting out, but she stayed on her hands and knees in the Sweet William and dwarf delphiniums. Henry went up on the porch for the milk crate, brought it over, and sat on it behind where Arlene was weeding. "Looks like you're getting dirty," he said.

"Oh, yeah. I think your son is down in the machine barn."

"I'm here to talk to you."

"Oh." She lifted, sat back on her heels, pushed the hair out of her eyes with her wrist.

"Keep at what you're doing. I don't know what to say anyway."

"Having a tough day, old man?"

He swallowed, traced a long oval with his head, but wouldn't look at her. His eyes were red-rimmed and welling. "Keep at what you're doing," he demanded.

She obeyed, went back to the stringy-rooted plantain, taprooted dandelions and campion and cheeses, creeping Charley tacked down at every node—plickety-plick it said when she stripped it loose.

"How you bearing up?" he asked finally.

"I'm pretty numb, Henry."

"You ever break down?"

"Not if I can help it."

"No, neither does Lenora. What's your secret? Why couldn't it a been me, Arlene? I've had my run. He sold the cows, leased out all that work, and then this?"

She tried sitting back again. "I don't know, Henry."

"Don't look at me. I'm a mess. I can't sleep, can't eat, can't even goddamn drink."

"You should take something, Henry. Have Harold Snelling prescribe something."

"What's he doing with himself, Arlene?"

"I think he's just trying to live regular days, do regular stuff, with naps stuck in between." She stops weeding, stays on all fours, speaks to the ground. "I think he wishes he hadn't leased out the hayfields. Retiring wasn't something he was any good at anyway, and now he says it's just like waiting around for somebody to phone or something. Or come and get him. So he doesn't know whether or not to start anything that takes more than a day. You want a handkerchief?" she asked.

"No. Does he say anything about all the snits I had when he let the cows go?"

"No. He knows how hard this is on you."

"Goddamn it, Arlene, it's all I can do to see him. I want to hug him right through me, take his goddamn pancreas and jump in the river. Don't. Don't look at me."

She went back on her hands, plucking out tough little weeds. "You going down to the barn?" she asked finally.

"I can't." She heard him get up, his crying turning into little yelps. He put the crate back on the porch. He went back to his car, walking bent, a wire-figure that had been crumpled, mashed by some adolescent fit of temper.

# 4.

Nate and Jenny came in the back door. Jenny was whispering something. She would be six in a week. Arlene leaned back, peeked around the refrigerator. "What're you sneaking around about?"

"We brought you something, Grandma."

"What did you bring me?"

Jenny's face gathered around her mouth and nose, a belligerent smirk. She had something in her hands, hidden in the crouch of her body. Nate was checking the soles of his boots. "Don't worry about that," she told him. "I'm about to mop."

"Don't you want to know?" Jenny cried.

"Of course I do, but what's it going to take to get you to show me?"

With that, Jenny thrust out both hands, her face stretched vertically, as if waiting for a firecracker to go off. A toad squirmed, levered with little hands and arms at the sides of Jenny's fingers.

"Oh, my goodness." Arlene threw her hands up in mock terror. Jenny's laughter was a whinny.

"All right," Nate said. "Go put him back in the garden." He wouldn't look at Arlene.

"Let me keep him, Dad. I can keep him in my room. I want to take care of him."

"No. Put him back in the garden."

"Dad—"

"No."

Her lower lip thrust out fat and pendant, she sulked her way out the door. Nate's blunt gaze bounced off empty parts of the walls. "What's going on, Nate?"

He put his hands on his hips, stared at the floor.

"Shelby?" she said.

"Isn't back from Wind Flat. She was coming home last night."

"Sit down. Want some coffee?"

"No." He shuffled past, sat slumped at the table.

"She call you yesterday?"

"No."

"You don't know how she did?"

He shook his head.

Shelby rodeoed. She was a barrel racer and a pole bender. Nate was not a horseman. She rode, and he logged. He had his own logging truck, a cat, and a small portable mill.

Jenny came back in. "Whyn't you go back out?" Nate asked. "Out on the swings or something."

"I don't want to." She frowned at both of them. It was as if she'd been assigned to keep them from talking about bad things.

"Here," Arlene took a basket from atop the refrigerator and gave it to her. "Go fetch the eggs."

"I don't want to."

"Jenny," Nate said. He spoke softly, gravely.

"You and your dad can take a carton of eggs when you go," Arlene told her.

Still grimacing, Jenny took the basket and went out.

"What are you going to do, Nate?"

"I don't know." He still hadn't met her eyes.

"You don't think there's any way this is going to work, do you? People never change that much, not in a hunk as big as she'd need to."

"You can say that?" He squinted at her then. "You can just say that about anybody?"

"Pretty much I can."

"Pretty much you can." He nods, keeps on nodding, a kind of reverberating.

"Would it work better if I tried to defend her?"

"Work better?" He spaced the words. Warned her.

"What do you need me to do, Nate?"

"I don't need you to do anything," he whispered.

"Yes, you do. You need me to tell you to let her go." She made a hiss, sucking in a breath, the noise of turmoil, of labor. "Or you think you need me to tell you to hang on. Which one, Nate?"

"Jesus Christ!" he yelled, stood.

"Nate."

"Jesus Christ!" he yelled again.

She hugged him then. But she was making a judgment. She wasn't ever going to tell him to hang on. She couldn't. Shelby, Shelby. They all said she treated her horses good, which would've been terrific if Nate and Jenny were barn animals.

When Jenny came back, she opened the door, then closed it again, waited outside with her basket of seven eggs.

# 5.

Having knocked at her door, he stood hang-dog at the top of the steps. His ill-fitting vest of faded hunter orange, not much more than a gaudy tie-on rag, made him look like a child playing dress-up. It was the season of orange, when men and boys all stamped with the same bright color terrorized the countryside for five weeks. On rare occasions, a horse, mule, or cow fell to their prowess; llamas with their somewhat wild profile had to be painted orange or collared with a bell. In dry seasons, untended campfires at hunting camps burned acres of prairie and forest. Hunters left gates open or parked locked vehicles in front of them or blazed away at a herd of elk and sent the animals hurtling through successive sets of five-wire fencing, ripping out quarter-mile segments at every line. Boom boom boom, the guns sounded skyline to skyline from the weekend before Halloween to the Sunday after Thanksgiving. On a dark Monday dawn it was over, and a profound stillness settled again like snow; one small blessing for the months of gloom ahead.

She opened the door. "Yes?" There were two certainties about this scenario of a hunter at her door: he was there to ask for something, and he wasn't going to get it.

"I shot an elk, a cow, on Clary Creek, but I only crippled her. She crossed your fence, and I followed her. I found her on a bed and shot her, but she's on your land."

"In the safety zone?"

"Yes, ma'am." He was in his forties, at least, a graying mustache, white sideburns, short hair, strong blue eyes that didn't edge away.

"You broke the law." She waited, but he didn't deny it. "You don't shoot in a safety zone. What good's a safety zone? How would you like to live with high-powered rifles blasting away in the neighborhood of your bedroom?"

"I couldn't leave her to die. I didn't want her to suffer. I didn't want the meat wasted."

"What the coyotes or bears get is a waste?"

"I couldn't do it. I couldn't just leave her to die."

"Then you gutted her?"

"I did."

"There's no blood on you." Most hunters looked like they'd bathed in blood, especially with an elk, plaques of red like baked mud on the hair of the arms running at times up to their shoulders, maroon patches on their knees and on the toes of their boots.

He looks at his hands and wrists. "I washed it off in the snow."

"Two guys I turned in last year told me they were following a cripple. I get that story all the time. What they had were fresh tracks, or they chased them over the fence, or saw them there, and snuck in. They got fined good, lost their licenses."

Elk were the worst; they drove these weekend mountain men off their rockers. Once on the highway, on the way to Armstead, she was following a line of hunters' rigs—it was Sunday afternoon and everybody was on their way home–when all their brake lights went on. They pulled off, or halfway pulled off with their tailgate butts still out in the lane, several leaving their doors open. Out came the guns. Fumbling, running, they stopped at the fence and blazed away at a small herd of elk that had just crossed the highway. Arlene saw two cow-elk fall. She was out of her truck by then, too, yelling. "You can't shoot from the highway. And that's posted land." The eight to ten firing away ignored her. She got out a pencil and a notepad, scribbled down five plate numbers, drove to the Eighty-Eight Bar and called Fish and Game. They sent several wardens, but by the time they got there, the hunters were gone. They found one dead elk, and the drag marks of two that were taken ungutted, and although all the vehicles had been identified, no one was ever arrested or ticketed. They all denied it. There was no proof. Arlene got into an argument with a warden, but had to be satisfied with the explanation that they didn't have the resources to pursue anything that wasn't red-handed or more than a one-time infraction. After that, she kept a disposable camera in the jockey box. What could be worse than letting slobs walk?

"I can show you the blood track," the hunter on her step offered.

She looked off over his shoulder. "Did you walk or drive here."

"Walked."

"Where's your gun?"

"With the elk."

"I'll take you to your truck. I want your plate numbers anyway."

"You can have them now. I just want you to know, no matter how this comes out, I would do it again. I won't leave a wounded animal."

"You can show me that blood track too, then." She watched for a reaction but got nothing telltale.

In her truck, she said, "Maybe we write on the safety-zone signs that if you want to hunt in this zone, all you have to do is send in a cripple."

"I understand your position. I wouldn't like it either. I suppose that this has happened to you more than once."

She gaped at him.

"Yeah," he said. "But I wasn't hunting along your fence line. Where I shot her was more than a mile from that boundary. She made a beeline for your place, where she knew it was safe. She was hit in the neck and went down, but she got back up and got into the timber. She lost a lot of blood, so I don't understand it."

Arlene kept glancing at him through half-lidded eyes. "Where is she?"

In the creek bottom, maybe two hundred yards from your last hayfield."

"By the old homestead?"

"Yeah, right, there's an apple tree there."

"How do I know you didn't backtrack, smear some blood?"

He frowned disbelief. She waited. He looked away from her, out his window at the plane of white. "Backtrack?" he said finally. She waited. "Look," he said, "there are places, clearings where I could see tracks quite a ways ahead, and I cut across, made shortcuts."

"Good."

He stared out the window, didn't say anything, his head and expression locked. They remained silent for a mile or two. "What are you going to do? If that makes a difference? I mean when you find out I'm telling the truth?" There was something testy, a little challenging in the tone.

She glared at him. "I was home minding my own business, all right? And now you're in my truck on your way to your illegal elk on my land. I have every right to my suspicion. And I have an obligation."

He got out, opened and closed the three wire gates for her, and at the last gate turned the hub on his side to get it in the four-wheel. The snow was seven or eight inches deep with patches of ice in the low spots. When they crossed the hayfield, she still didn't know what she was going to do if there was a blood trail. No blood trail, and he was toast. Except she knew there was a blood trail. She'd been home watching a Broncos game. Now she was here, where there would be no good ending.

There was blood everywhere in the snow around the animal, pools with purple clots where he opened her, slashes of red where he laid out the liver and the heart, and then all the patches and blots where he must have washed up in the snow. He'd skinned around the neck and down the shoulders, pushed the hide out with sticks, and he had her propped open wide to cool. Arlene looked at the neck, the bloody hole, and then inside at the ribs, the killing shot there. The inside was clean of hair and blood, even the tenderloins. "How'd you get her so clean?"

"I carry a washrag. I washed her good with snow."

Arlene looked around again at the bloody snow everywhere. She could see where he'd wrung the rag. She considered the big animal again, her unmistakably feminine face, large eyes and ears, small well-shaped nose. He hadn't cut off the teats, a trickle of milk necklaced a bluish membrane. "The calf was with her?"

"There were three others. I assume one was her calf, but I didn't watch them. I was so focused on her, trying to make sure I didn't lose her."

She went back to the neck. The coarse, dark hair was tarred with blackened blood. "How do you shoot her in the neck without killing her?"

"God, I don't know." He pulled off his orange cap, brushed back his hair with the back of his wrist. "Missed every bone, missed the big arteries and veins. How do you do that?"

That was her question. "Let's load her. I don't want another truck in here."

He brightened. She glared back, but didn't say anything. I never asked for this power, she was thinking. I didn't want it. You did this.

At one point, when they were cradling the forequarters, the drooping neck and head, his eyes met hers, and there was something grateful showing, the way dogs look when they want affection. She moved her eyes down to his chin and attached there as they struggled trying to get the lower leg over the tailgate, then the head. They were both gasping when they got the carcass to a position where Arlene could wedge herself against it, manage alone for a moment, whereupon he vaulted into the truck, grasped the elk's ears, and in a series of lunges, edged the animal forward. Arlene pushed behind at the hindquarters, but she couldn't lift them. When they hit the stopping point of that maneuver, he leaped down and sidled up alongside her. In twin efforts, their bodies pressed side to side, they lifted, heaved, and slid the elk on into the bed.

"Wow," he said breathless. "Thank you."

No, she was thinking. She had her hands on her thighs, and she wouldn't look at him.

"Oh, you got blood on you," he cried, rushed her with a gob of snow, scraped at her shoulder and below, moving dangerously, mindlessly close to her breast. She didn't push him away. She watched his eyes until he glanced up at her.

When he got back into the truck at the last gate, she told him that she was going to report him, that they'd slide the elk into his truck from hers, but that he'd have to give the animal up at the checking station.

"That's the way it goes," he said, looking straight ahead, saying it like a recitation, what he'd memorized and couldn't go back on. He left it at that. They said nothing about the elk again. She didn't know what else they would take away from him, his gun, his license, his rights to hunt for so many years, maybe nothing but the elk. She didn't want to know. It wasn't her doing. She was the outside party. By the time she got home, the deal would be over.

It was, and it wasn't. She felt as if she had done something wrong, when she hadn't. She went by the rules. What was more useless than regret? Over the kitchen sink, she rinsed away the last trace of the elk blood from her coat, but she could still feel him, his hand scrubbing at her.

# The Deer Walking
# Upside Down

The weather? How do you argue about that? This was nothing about money or alcohol or Clayton, their son-in-law. Or trivia—whether, say, Eugene McCarthy ever really supported Reagan. On this winter day, he'd maundered aloud about the heat of last summer, wondered idly if it got over a hundred out on the lake.

"Why wouldn't it?" she slung back. He tried to explain.

When did she conclude that everything he said was bogus? Once, there was an occasional butting of heads, maybe an interval of knee-jerk reactions before descending to the steady toe-to-toe, but this hadn't seemed gradual like that. It came more like an epiphany, except what do you call an epiphany when it's bullshit?

So the lake is a different place?" she chased.

"It's a heat sink, for Christ's sake."

"They should give two different weather forecasts. Today in Fletcher, it will be a hundred, but take your parkas out on the lake. You're saying wind doesn't mix it, even?"

"No, just not as much as you might think."

"As much as you think, though, that's what it does." She lowered her voice, thinned her eyes, so that she could see all the way through to the back of his eyeballs, where she snapped up the shades, flung the sashes open. The trouble was that it wasn't the wind she was thinking about or even cared about, she was simply skeptical of anything that passed through his mind. The Great Corrupter. If they had become two blind people describing an elephant, their orbits posted forever to opposite ends of the beast:

*"That won't hold more than two quarts."*
*"It holds a gallon, Larry."*

*"In* Mississippi Masala, *the one who played the father. That's who it was, Larry."*
*"No, not Nehru, he didn't play Nehru in the* Gandhi *I saw. They didn't even look alike."*
*"Yes. Rosh something."*

*"Merrit is not a day over fifty five,"* Carol affirmed.
*"He's over sixty. And it's Merrick."*
*"The superintendent's name is Merrit, not Merrick."*
*"You can't believe Ron Merrick is in his fifties,"* Larry inveighed. *"He's a grandfather, for Christ's sake."*
*"There are lots of grandfathers in their fifties, and it's not Ron either."*
*"So what is it?"*
*"Something Merrit. I can't remember."*
*"All you know is that I'm wrong."*
*"Odds are."*

Odds are that Carol and he are driving to his brother's place. Behind these thousand bickering hills on the horizon, Larry imagines dark, lost canyons. The best that could be said at the moment is that they aren't yelling, as they had the night before after they'd gone out to dinner. What scared him most was that they could live together in the same house, sleep in the same bed, kiss each other good night or more—take it all the way, sometimes—and still be on the outside looking in. They lived in entwined but separate channels. At home they could retreat to different rooms, but in the car on trips neither could flee, every escape valve rusted shut. Now they could add going out to dinner to this list of dreads?

She's brought up the oil change. "You said every three thousand miles, and suddenly when you forget to do it, forty-five hundred is okay."

"I didn't forget. We put on two thousand of those miles on the interstate, which makes it different." They'd driven to Seattle for her niece's wedding. What was their mileage there and back? How many fights per mile? How many sinkholes of silence?

"What makes it different is you forgetting and not wanting to admit it."

"You won't believe me. Look at it from the crankshaft's point of view. That's what counts. It's in the middle of the motor, where the oil goes. When you're not driving in town and shifting down all the time, the crank turns fewer times for every mile."

"Different rules for you, that's all I hear. You should teach them at Quik-Lube that their numbers need to be changed. They could put them up on the wall. Larry's rules. Except they're no good unless your name is Larry."

He doesn't say anything. Down it comes, this screen, like a stage curtain falling between them. "What's happened?" he asks abruptly. "I don't know how to make this stop."

"What's not stopped?"

"What we're doing. Do we hate each other?"

"Sometimes. It's your crankshaft, I think."

"Right," he says.

"It is. You know how to rile me, and you won't pass a good shot when you see it."

"As if you pass the shots you get."

"You don't know how many I let go by. You don't know how careful I have to be." Her voice drops dramatically.

"Careful? That's an interesting concept. Pampered, that's how I should feel?"

"What were we talking about before? When we left? Wasn't it your brother?"

"We agree about my brother."

"No, not the religion. The way he treats Rosalie. Like she's a complete pinhead."

"She doesn't treat him any better."

"No, but she doesn't use him for a rug."

"They don't fight any more than we do."

"I don't know why they stay together."

He doesn't say anything to this.

"Stuck. They've quit on each other."

He tries to divine where she's headed.

"I don't like being talked down to any more than she does."

"I talk down to you more than you do to me?"

"Only all the time. In everything, you make it seem that I'm the one who doesn't understand The Big Picture." She says the last three words with a deep voice. "That I'm the one who never sees beyond her nose. While you take in universes. You belong on the ceiling of the Sistine Chapel. Your finger would have to be longer, that's all."

"Yeah, well, you refuse to look an inch past your own nose. You're the arrogant one, the one who believes it's all common sense, so long as it's your version of common sense. But it's changed, you know, how much you've thought I'm wrong. Once, it was now and then. Now, it's always. Does that make me narrow and you open-minded?"

"It's different than that."

"I see," he says.

"There, that's what I mean. You don't see. There's the sarcasm that's supposed to make it clear to me how messed up I am about everything."

"And I'm not messed up about everything if you think I'm wrong about everything I say?"

"In a different way."

"I see."

Carol takes half a breath and holds it. When he doesn't hear her breathing aloud again, he assumes it's a tactic, as if silent breathing is twice as condemning as mere silence.

She parks the car behind his brother's—a little close, he thinks, but says nothing. She says, "Let's get through this."

He can feel his eyes bulge. He thrusts his canted head toward her.

"This dinner, I mean."

He lifts away. "Right." He sweeps to his skyward post, viewing himself from above in the right miniaturized context, as a blinking mite, one of so many billion tricked creatures on the skin of one of a bajillion planets.

Rosalie is in the kitchen staring at the wall, rigid and erect as she winds on the salad spinner. She softens and smiles at them, the spinner winds down, diminuendo. In the adjoining room, Mel crawls out of his La-Z-Boy when Larry wishes him a happy birthday, nods with bulky motions like a horse, and says thanks.

"Mom's not here?" Larry asks.

"She wasn't ready." Mel looks at his watch. "Maybe by now."

Rosalie sighs. "I told him she'd be ready by the time he got there."

Mel lurches, frowns, throws Larry a knowing look, then sags. "Want a beer?"

"I'll go get her," Larry says. "I've still got my coat on." He ducks back into the kitchen. "You need anything?" he asks.

Rosalie squints, searches the ceiling blindly, then shakes her head. Carol is pouring herself a glass of wine. Mel wanders in. "She'd be here now," Rosalie says.

"It's his birthday. He doesn't have to do anything," Larry tells her. "Do you need anything?"

"Then it must be his birthday every day."

"Put a lid on it, Rosalie," Mel snarls. "They didn't come over to listen to you bellyache." He says *bellyache* like a caller for a square dance.

Mel goes to the refrigerator. Larry catches Carol's gaze, her eyes hard as a spider's. A chill of recognition? This kitchen is a web, with all these cob-dusty snares.

Larry flees out to the car, where for a moment he contemplates the house, a blue box that Mel and Rosalie live in. Their kids are gone, off to their own boxes. Karen, too, his and Carol's daughter, off to another city. Are there webs starting in the box where Karen and Clayton live, tentacles that scare Karen? Is it universal, accumulations in every box that one must tear down, chop away, lest one day they metastasize? Or is it a personal situation? Are he and Carol, like Mel and Rosalie, the opposite of star-crossed lovers? Star-splayed? Posted at the far ends of an ever-expanding, an ever-more-unknowable universe?

Larry drives the back way, through the ten- and twenty-acre lots, the cropping checkerboard developments of houses all struck from the same template, then back again into the lots and past the cemetery, a golf course, the occasional sugar-beet field. It's early December, the ground frozen half gray with sanded white spots of snow in the dips and basins. Geese and mule deer, a pheasant or two, fleck the barrenness. The two-lane pavement is narrow with steep borrow pits, the speed limit a default fifty-five even where hedges and lawns and barbecues and the strewn array of bikes and sleds crowd up against the indifferent, contemptuous traffic. Sprawl has a way of being recent and old at the same time.

Where the gray sky opens out again, under a fence row of old cottonwood, Larry sees a buck walking slowly toward the road. A three-point. It's the tail-end of the rut, and a few bucks from the surrounding rims and cedar breaks still poke about in the valley. This deer walks with his head down, as if dogging a scent, but he seems in no particular hurry. Larry passes by, broods on, his unhappiness parked like an unwanted passenger in the backseat.

Unaccountably, a quarter mile on, the deer thrusts himself back into Larry's mind. What's true about a deer is that there is no more beautiful animal on the earth. There couldn't be, because there's no surpassing what's perfect. He glances up at the rearview mirror to see in startling clearness a slow-motion sequence of the deer walking over the highway and a white car approaching. The slow, deliberate clarity of the buck's progress is confounded by an absurd geometry of a path arcing above the highway and the swerving car—the deer is walking there upside down, as he would if he were decorating the outer edge of stationery or a quilt or weaving. Larry blinks and the deer is gone, but he can tell by a glimpse of the white car's side and by the boat-like lift and fall of the chassis it's an old American model, a Continental or a Cadillac, maybe. The driver appears to stop on the narrow shoulder.

In another quarter mile, Larry turns left on an intersecting road. Going on, glancing over his shoulder now and then with this diagonal view across an intervening field, he sees the car starting up again and driving on. A van that had stopped behind follows now. Must be dead, Larry thinks. The image keeps playing: the deer walking upside-down...what, three or four feet above the car? That animal wasn't watching. Nor the driver. Not enough.

There was the buck, intact and solid, walking right-side-up on frozen ground, mindful of a scent maybe; then he was upside-down, still walking, except not for long and forever.

Larry can see his mother at her window when he pulls up. Maybe she can recognize his car, maybe not. Walking up the sidewalk, he waves. She's squinting, tilting at the window, but she doesn't respond. He knocks and goes in.

"It's me," he says.

"Ah, Larry, everything okay? I've been waiting." She has her coat on, her bag with her oxygen canister. He tells her that all is well. "Will you run to the desk and check me out?" She pulls off the plastic tubes that feed to her nose and turns off the machine.

When he returns, she's standing in the hall. She takes his arm and—slowly, walking haltingly the way people do in lines—they make their way to his car. The series of maneuvers and stages she goes through to seat herself in the car are remarkably precise yet pathetic at the same time. "Is the birthday boy okay?" she asks, when he pulls out onto the highway. "I was expecting *him*."

"Doing fine." He glances at her, finds her examining him with her eyes moving like sea anemones, soft and waving and searching. Macular degeneration well advanced.

"Well, this will be nice," he says, wincing at the nothingness he's just expressed.

"What I'd like to do is beat you at a game of cribbage. That's what I miss most about these get-togethers." She's staring ahead now, and Larry wonders how much of the road ahead she can make out. "Especially Rosalie—she's the most fun to beat. And you."

"You didn't always beat me."

"But you were the most fun to muggins."

"Yeah." He wouldn't play muggins cribbage with anybody else. He could deal with losing points he missed, but it stuck in him sideways when his opponent got to take what he missed. If he was too serious, his only comfort was that it was no less true for Carol. "I'm sorry," he says to his mother, "that you can't play cribbage anymore."

"Or smoke. And that's the one I'll never get over."

"You don't want to get over it."

"No, I don't."

There were different kinds of regrets. If his mother was sorry she couldn't play cribbage or smoke, she wasn't sorry she had smoked, even though it brought her to this. She could take getting mugginsed from anybody, although he couldn't remember it ever happening.

"I saw a deer get hit on the way over."

"Oh no…Was it awful?"

"I saw it from a distance. It's just up ahead here."

But when they drive by, he can't see the deer's body in the borrow pit. It didn't seem possible that an animal knocked that high into the air could live or walk any distance away to die. They go on another mile before Larry brakes and turns into a driveway. "I've got to go back," he tells his mother. "I need to know."

"Of course. You didn't see it when we passed?"

"I didn't."

Returning, he pulls off just across from the line of cotton-woods, his marker for where the deer had been. He has to park deep in the borrow pit to get off the road completely. The car tilts badly, and he has to hold the steering wheel to stay in place. His mother is pressed into the corner by the door, which she resists with an elbow. Everything seems out of whack: no deer anywhere, the car's slant alarming, his mother here. But she says nothing.

He leans to see out his side. Those are the trees where the deer crossed. He cranes about.

"Oh Jesus, shit," he blurts, for the deer is only fifty yards ahead of them, alive and struggling. The buck lifts his head out of the tall grass, thrashes, and falls back. One of his antlers is gone. All four legs must be broken, or his back; he can't get off his side. "Shit, shit, shit," Larry moans. He's been alive all this time. What's it take to kill an animal like that?

"Is it there?" His mother squirms, strains leaning toward the windshield. "Alive?"

"Yes. Lying in the grass. And I don't have anything."

"Can he live?"

"No, I can't imagine how he's lasted this long. Goddammit, dammit, dammit." He freezes, holds the sides of his face with both hands. The tire iron would not be enough. A rock, not enough. He has no knife, no gun. A rock, it's not enough, he tells himself a second time. He starts the car, stretches up to see behind, then revs it to shoot back up onto the road.

"What are you going to do?"

"I have to get something to kill him with." He accelerates.

"To Mel's?"

"No. That'll take a half hour. That deer's been there that long already. Shit," he hisses.

She doesn't say anything about his swearing. A small white house appears on the left. As he brakes and turns in, his mother does not intrude with questions. He strides to the porch. The steps are creaky, old wood, the structure itself peeling paint, the windows obscured with plastic nailed under furring strips. Larry pounds on the doorframe. He can see into the kitchen; it's lit, but no response. He knocks again, this time on the door itself, the glass amplifying the staccato racket.

A shirtless man appears carrying a baby, opens the door at once. Round face, short dark hair, a day's growth of a dark beard, the wakeful yet silent baby with light skin but the same dark eyes and swatch of hair. The man's expression is questioning, though without any apparent suspicion.

"I'm sorry to bother you," Larry says, "but a car just hit a deer just back there, and I want to put it out of its misery. Do you have a knife I could borrow?"

"I have a knife," he says tentatively. "Come in. It's not a very sharp knife."

He speaks with the hint of an accent; Larry guesses he's Mexican. The house is warm, humid, the light inside incandescent yellow. Something in a lidded pot cooks on the stove. The man rattles through drawers, the baby watching his face. "I saw the car. It was an old man. But he drove on. Here. I'm sorry, but this is not a very good knife."

Larry examines it. "Oh, boy," he murmurs. The knife has a blade as long as his hand but it's incredibly dull and the point is rounded. "Do you...?"

The man shrugs.

"A steel then, or a stone?"

He rifles again in a second drawer, hands Larry a whetstone the size and shape of a cube of butter. Larry thanks him and rushes back out to the car. He starts the car, then sits there whetting the blade. "Did you get what you need?" his mother asks.

"It's really dull."

She doesn't say anything, seems to apprehend that he needs to concentrate, get another plan or gather his forces. He drives back, pulls off across from the deer and, taking both the stone and the knife, bolts across the road.

Vainly, the deer struggles upward. Larry drops the stone, clutches the single antler and tries to force the deer's head back onto the ground, but the broken animal is remarkably strong, so Larry has to lean in and throw his weight over him. He uses both hands to get the head down, then lifts his fist high and drives the knife at the neck. The blade bends, nearly doubles back, but does not penetrate. The deer convulses, flings Larry's hand away and flops about but cannot rise.

Leaning back, Larry chokes. Stupidly, he straightens the defective blade, examines the point. Only a grinder can put a point on this. In mad, jabbing motions, he works the nearly straightened blade on the whetstone again. He's heard stories about tornadoes impaling power poles with grass stems. Can he persuade his arm to channel the power of a storm? He has the deer's head down again, and this time he plunges the blade with the fullest concentration of force and speed he can summon. The blade goes in to the handle. In frantic, spastic lunges, he saws the blade up and down, outward. Purple-red blood gushes, fills the hole made by the knife, mounds out and over in a heavy, syrupy column. In one motion, Larry lunges back, pulls the knife out, and rises. He averts his face from the deer's, fetches the stone from where he dropped it, a couple feet away.

At the highway's edge, he wipes his hands and the knife in long, frosty stems of grass. He doesn't look back.

In the car, his mother remains quiet. He appreciates her respect.

"It's done," he whispers.

At the house, the man still cradles his baby, but now he has a shirt on. From the doorway, Larry extends the knife, handle first, and then the stone. "Thank you."

The man, like Larry's mother, does not ask, but his eyes shine questioningly. Larry shows the man the palms of his hands, attempts an apologetic shake of the head that comes off more like a shudder.

At Mel and Rosalie's, Larry walks his mother in and then goes to the bathroom to sit on the lid of the toilet, while his mother tells them what happened.

"Wow," Mel says when Larry comes back out, "you've already put in a day. Where's your hunter orange?"

"Yeah." Larry doesn't look at them.

"I'm sorry," Carol says, "that you had to do that."

"It's a good thing you were there," says Rosalie, "or who knows how long he would've had to suffer."

"He'd still be there waiting to die," Mel adds.

Larry broods: Suffer? What a strange word. It could be waafer, poofer, laffer. A funny-sounding word for the most peculiar thing. Pain, certainly, but that could have been the smallest part. A lens of fear, the deer's and his own, fused into a single column clear as ice, when neither wanted it.

In the kitchen, they watch him.

"I see you as God's instrument," Mel says.

"I feel like I'm somebody's instrument."

"You were," Mel says, ever more fervent. "Don't you think?"

"You don't want to know what I'm thinking, Mel."

They wait for him to elaborate, but he says nothing.

"You're upset, Larry," his mother says.

"Yep," he says.

"Well, I'm glad the deer's out of his misery," Mel says.

Larry won't look at him.

Frowning, Mel picks at the back of his hand the way he does when he's uncomfortable. At length, he rises. "Come on, Mom, let's go see if the game's started."

She stands in stages, untangles her oxygen tubes. "Larry," she says, touching his shoulder, "you only did what you could do."

He touches her hand. "I know, Mom."

Rosalie goes back to the kitchen, but Carol stays. "You seem a little deranged to me, Larry."

He regards her, uncertain whether she intends any accusing. "I know. I think I want to be."

"But you're okay?"

He opens his hands, shows them and his complete bewilderment to her. He widens his eyes and blinks.

"Oh," she says. "Yes."

He considers this: her understanding is a kind of affection, his to have. A gift, but he needs to keep it a small one. He dares not be too grateful. Today, he saw a deer walking in a place he has to keep track of.

# RECLAMATIONS

Whoever is in charge of Johnny's calamities—earth, fate, God— has a fondness for September. Four years ago, two weeks after 9/11, his favorite dog of all time, a seven-year-old lab in the prime of his life, chased a pheasant across the county road, got hit by a truck, and died curled up in a culvert. Three years before that Johnny's ex-wife was diagnosed with breast cancer, node involvement. Two years before that she'd left him, and nine years before that his infant daughter, Jasa, almost died of an intussusception, a telescoped intestine.

Now this September: as a sophomore safe at the university, Jasa's applying for a job as an accompanier in Guatemala. Accompanier is a word his dictionary rightfully excludes, a made-up word, a hand-holding euphemism for a witness-protection program. Johnny's daughter has volunteered to live among 150 witnesses to village genocide, testifiers that the accused powers would like to snuff. Jasa's small presence is supposed to make that more difficult.

Jasa? Jesus Christ.

And of course this is when bears return to plunder. For September is their month, too, although ravages can leak into October, if these marauders get thwarted from anything they wanted but didn't get in September. So bears, of all things, are what he brings up when Ramona from the Tribal Lands arrives. She's there with the morning sun, eight on the nose, just like she said, so he hasn't had time to clean up the mess, to clean out the culprit he's just discovered.

"Bear?" she says.

"Yeah, or I would've been ready. I've got the papers you sent right here." He's rustling in his desk. She stands in the doorway. "Coffee, you want coffee?"

"The bear is still here?"

"Yeah, I was just about to blast him."

"Blast him?"

Johnny stops digging, rubs his face with one hand, pauses the hand over his nose and eyes as if it were a curtain that might change the scene. "You want him?" he asks. "You can have him."

"Where is he?"

"In the backyard. About a hundred feet up in a ponderosa."

"Can I see him?"

"Sure. I'll see if I can get him down for you."

"How do you do that?" Her waist-length black hair ripples down, waves left behind, he's thinking, from braids she's just un-plaited. She has a wonderful nose, with an arc that reflects the same filet-blade line of her stance: long and clean and easy, re-laxed but bright.

"I told you." He rises, goes to the corner behind the couch and draws out the gun.

"You're not doing that." Her voice skids.

"You're the one who wants to see him." He goes out the back-door.

She rushes behind. "Quit messing with me. I just wanted to see him."

"So there he is." Johnny points up. "Just below the top."

She shields her eyes with one hand. "I can't see. The dark part, you mean?"

He backs away from her, cracks the gun, slips in a shell. He backs farther until he has about an eighty-yard sighting of the bear's body humped around the tree. The bear's sitting on a limb, his head behind the trunk. She's right—there isn't much to see. Johnny aims and fires. The bear bolts upright, whoofs, stands on the limb, climbs to another above limb, and then backs down, still whoofing loudly. The pink of his mouth shows, the reflection from an eye. But he isn't going anywhere; Johnny can see that.

Ramona rushes at Johnny again, yelling about what he can't do, about reporting him. He breaks the gun slowly, slides out the empty shell. Ramona's open mouth is startlingly large, but it fits right with that nose, those long cheeks. She has a husky voice full of command and authentic rage. He holds up the shell. "What?" she shouts.

"Look...birdshot. It won't penetrate at this distance. Just stings."

Ramona's eyes glitter, her lips pressed tight, that large mouth clamped. She steps toward him. "Why are you trying to get my hackles up?"

"It's not you. I'd like to get him out of here."

"Why should he come down when you're shooting at him?"

"Seems sensible to me."

"But if he comes down, it only brings him closer to you and your gun."

Johnny's still thinking about her remark that he was doing this to raise her hackles.

"Leave him alone," she scolds. "He'll come down and leave, won't he?"

"I don't know."

"Why wouldn't he?"

"It's a little complicated."

"Complicated?"

He turns away. "You're here to arrange an easement, aren't you, not to defend my bears?"

She doesn't say anything, and they trail back into the house, stand on either side of the kitchen table. "People who want conservation easements," she observes, "aren't usually the type who shoot at bears."

"I'm not a type, and bears are a pain in the ass. You never said whether you wanted coffee."

"I'm all right."

"That means no?"

"Right. Is that your daughter?" She's looking at the picture taped to the side of the refrigerator, Jasa walking on her hands on the flower garden path, nasturtiums up to her elbows. He nods, turns, runs water in the teakettle and puts it on the stove. "She's at the U."

There's a long gap. "You must be proud," she says finally, softly.

"Why's that?" He turns to look at her, catches what looks like a dusting of pain. She sharpens, gathers, but it's lousy cover for this blast that's hit her from somewhere. "How about a piece of pie?" he follows.

"Pie?"

He turns, studies her. He's lived on the rez thirty years now, enough time to culture a decent appreciation for the reticence common to many of his neighbors, a reticence he may have once confused with indifference. "Raspberry pie."

"All right," she says.

"So maybe you'll go for coffee now that you got pie on the way?"

Maybe she doesn't like the playing, or maybe she does. He sees her mouth move, a flicker she can't hide. "All right," she says again.

He goes to the fridge. "Go ahead," he says, "lay out your stuff.

Give me your spiel. I'm listening."

She complies, pulling up a chair and opening out her folder. "First thing," she says, "this easement obligates the tribe to make sure what you donate stays donated. So long after both of us are gone, the tribe has to go on as protector. Which means they don't want to take on something like that unless the donation is worth all the trouble."

"You want my house, too?" He licks the knife after he's made his cut. She watches on until he puts it in the sink, goes for the spatula.

"Quit jabbing at everything I say," she says. "No more development, or not much anyway. We'd have to agree to a limit. That's the point, of course: no subdividing, and it has to stay one-family. No commercial logging, no mining, and no grazing since the acreage isn't that large and the river bottom is so sensitive. You don't have livestock anyway, do you?"

"Just bears." The pot whistles. He pours the water in the press, gives her a fork and a slice of pie on his red Fiestaware, sits, and then gets up again for napkins.

"We'd like to stipulate what the place can be used for—economically, I mean. Bed and breakfast that sort of thing."

"Nope, not that one. I saw that in those attachments you sent, but I can't do that. No stipulations on how to make a living. The rest I'll do, but whoever's here has to make a living, and it isn't right for me to lock them out of situations I can't even imagine. You'll have to figure out if the rest is enough. That and the easement on the road I don't have yet."

"The lane in, you mean?"

He likes the way she holds her head up only partway, lifts her eyes so that her gaze ricochets off her brow. "Yeah," he says, "that access. It's revocable. They got all the papers and stuff for a regular one, but I haven't heard a thing. It isn't supposed to be any problem. I give you all the development rights, and you give me a road easement. I think they forgot, that's all. They built me the road, for Christ's sake. If you can figure that out."

So Indian, this whole thing. When he bought the place thirty-four years ago, the white guy who sold it to him had cut gate wires twice, which anybody from here ought to know is akin to pulling a gun. When Johnny drove in to spend his first night on his place, he just happened to meet Vic Big Legs along the fence line. Vic wasn't the sort of Indian he expected. This guy was in his seventies, a dapper man who wore slacks and a fedora. In the years after, Johnny never saw Vic dressed any other way. That afternoon, Vic's tiny, gray-haired wife was sitting in a polished sedan parked at the edge of the county road, watching out the window at Vic, who was driving fencing staples into a knot of barbed wire on the gate. He was locking off the bumpy and rutted lane that crossed the Jackson Sundown Rodeo Grounds to the land Johnny had just bought.

Vic's wife wouldn't meet Johnny's eyes when he walked past the car, and Vic wouldn't look up until the staple had been driven. "Hello," Johnny said and introduced himself. Vic glanced at him, picked a second staple off the top of a post, and set to driving it in behind the other. "I just bought the place below from Streeter," Johnny went on, "and this is the only way I've got of getting in."

"He cut the gate wire," Vic muttered, swinging precise chopping motions at the staple.

"I'm hoping we can work something out. I got to have some way to get in there."

"You go talk to the Council. This is Indi'n ground."

"I'd like to talk to you. For starters."

"You go see the council." Vic pointed at him with the back of the hammer, then he went round Johnny back to his car, and they drove off. That was on the weekend. Johnny left his pickup on the county road, walked in, taking his sleeping bag with him and sleeping with the mice in the well house. In the beginning, there wasn't much more than that, the well house and a small barn. The owners preceding Streeter had burned down the house during a New Year's Eve party. Streeter brought in a trailer and took it with him when he left. He'd never said anything about a feud over the lane. Johnny knew the access was revocable, but he couldn't see past the beauty of this ground: a small, clear river with a stone bottom, the banks lined with cottonwood and pine, juniper and red-oshier. Life is a risk.

Monday, after his first weekend on the place, Johnny went to the council and with little trouble secured the revocable ease-ment in his name. The four council members in attendance passed around a memo—a note from Vic, Johnny guessed—whereupon they granted access with the stipulation that Johnny and anybody going to his place promise to leave no gates open or cut any wire. Intent on being a good neighbor, Johnny figured he could, in time, earn his way into a full easement. Two decades dwindled by, but the tribe had no interest in giving anything away. Their business was in trying to eke back what the Dawes Act had stolen from them a century before when it opened the reservation to white settlement.

Then a winter of heavy snows four years ago changed every-thing. High-school kids got in the habit of going out to the rodeo grounds during the school lunch hour and driving spinout loops in their high-pocket pickups, carving out dirt-sprayed loops ev-erywhere, sliding into corrals, knocking down posts, and making general mayhem. One bunch flung bottles at the outdoor lights and broke out all the bulbs. In a swoop of reaction, the council decided to fence off a separate lane for Johnny on the east border of grounds, so they could lock off all other access.

On day one Johnny didn't know if he was getting locked out with the vandals, but by day two he had his own private lane. Moreover, somebody in administration said if they were to put in a new road, they'd do it right, so in the spring they sent out the Coyote Rocks Job Corp to bring in gravel, cut a new road cut over the edge, and do it to "specs." A crew and a team of young recruits with a dump truck, grader, and a cat, worked a month on it. Johnny asked the crew's supervisor if this meant he had an easement, too. Go to the land office, fill out the papers, and they'll issue you one, he said. Which Johnny did.

That was three years ago. Everybody seemed nice enough about it, but they never sent him anything. Just built a damn good road. For free and for nobody but him, a road with no papers. To hell with it, he'd decided. Let sleeping dogs lie. And he had until now, until he found out about conservation easements, this way of keeping the river like it was. Moreover, the arrangement gave him a sort of quid pro quo. Some of my rights for one of theirs.

Ramona takes notes on this short history. "I think I know where it got lost," she says. "Lands and the legal department are fighting. So some things got postponed."

He gets up, pours their coffee. "They aren't fighting over my road easement, are they?"

"No. I'll make sure it gets done." She says this with the solemnity of a hit man. He's impressed with the set of her jaw. In this vertigo of revelation, he's struck by the same fresh jolt he got in third or fifth grade or somewhere back then when another's eyes, another's response, first stood him on his head. He sits. She's going through her papers.

He asks, "You got a job with the tribe when? Five or ten years ago?"

She looks a little concerned, but he doesn't let her answer.

"Before that you went to the community college at the agency, and before that when you graduated or got your GED, you were already married so you had to wait." He could say she's got…what, one, two, three children? Because he can see things right now, can do more than guess, but he's already crossed a line, for she's lurched, flushed.

"I'm not here for this," Ramona says. If she were a deer, she'd run. But she can't. She's learned what everybody learns, how to be an adult at work. She got to ask about Jasa, he could say, and this is another quid pro quo, that's all. My story and yours. Except she's been burned, he can tell.

Once more, he feels this strange power of clairvoyance lift in him. He says, "My daughter's applying for a dangerous job in Guatemala. She wants my support and her mother's to do this, but her mother won't give it, I don't think. I want to help, but not just because my ex-wife won't. I think. I can't tell. I'd do whatever I could to stop her from going to Iraq, if that was the case. I'd do that."

Ramona's face has retreated a little, her lips parted. But he knows still that he's not wrong, that he hasn't misjudged.

Ramona asks, "What's her name?"

"Jasa."

"Jasa," she says.

"You have children?" They both know yes, that he's fishing for more.

She closes her lips but opens her jaws, lips stretching so as to smooth the crumpling away. She turns, stares off over one shoulder.

"I'm sorry," he says. "I'm a stupid hermit who doesn't know when to shut his mouth."

"He drove off Finley Creek Bridge. You've seen the cross there?" She doesn't wait for an answer. "Six years ago this month."

"This month." He retreats, stuffs his eyes in a corner so as to leave her alone. What he took for clairvoyance wasn't that at all.

He's described a prison. She's had no options. On the other hand, if she'd supposed a past for him, she would've had nothing to go on. He could've come from anywhere, gone anywhere. It was an obscenity, this difference in their pasts, their immediate and ulti-mate histories.

So where did this urge of his come from, to contain her, cir-cumscribe her? His ex-wife had said, so many years ago, that he didn't know how to live with uncertainty, that he would put things where they didn't go, just to get them in a box.

That's true, he admits, but he sure as hell didn't have any fran-chise on fear. It's Marilyn he's answering now. She won't let Jasa go, not if she can swing it. There are varieties of fear, just like there are varieties of himself. He glances at Ramona. And of her, of course, all the varieties he's just mashed to one lump. This in-stinct for stupidity is why he lives alone.

"Let's keep with this," she says, gestures at the papers. "So you won't accept any clause on the kind of business you want to keep off this place?"

Varieties of courage, too. That's what's on the other side of shit. You can turn damn near anything over, bad fortune or good, and find a different door to go through. He feels like a big ferry ramming the dock, the slow, unstoppable grinding and rending. Part of it is the way she speaks, how she moves those long fingers. It's not something he can keep from seeing. No rings on those fin-gers. There are so many things he can't keep from thinking.

"No," he says. "No clause on that. Taste that pie." How long's it been since he's had this much that needs thinking about. Let's keep this idiot in his box. "That doesn't have to be a deal breaker, does it?"

"I don't think so." She's cutting the tip off her pie. She looks at him before taking a bite. This is an appraisal, no question about it. Go ahead, he thinks, urges even, use that cookie cutter for men, it's only fair. He watches her lips, her teeth, red raspberries. He can taste her bite of pie better than his own.

"I'll have it written up the way I think it'll suit both of us. There'll be some legal clauses, some allowances on what you can still do, like cutting deadwood for firewood, that sort of thing. I've got to run it by my people, this part about no restriction on the sort of business. And then the road thing. But I don't think those will kill it. Then you read it over, and if it looks good we'll get it surveyed, put it all together, and set it up." She sips the coffee she didn't want. "I'll chase down this road easement."

He sits there filled with pounds and pounds of indiscriminate wonder.

"This is good," she says about the pie, but she's only filling the hole of his silence. "No, I mean it," she gropes.

He smiles at her, imagines her imagining him, guessing at his incoherence. He'll go to Guatemala to see Jasa. He'll do that. He could even ask Marilyn if she wanted to go with him, rent a car together there, because he could deal with that, too. The adults we are, just wear the word. Now and forever, all the way to the end.

She finishes off her pie, and with a little still in her mouth she asks if she could leave by the backdoor, see if the bear is still there.

"He's still there."

She nods, puts her papers away. "But it's all right to take another look? Without you blasting him, I mean?"

"Sure." They rise, and he follows her out the door. The bear sits on the same limb, but he's facing them this time, squashes down a little, huffs and whoofs when he sees them. He's peering down along one of his dangling legs. Johnny and Ramona stare back up. Johnny realizes his neck is getting sore from this depressing business, the invader lodged straight above. "Oh oh," she says. "Did he do that?" She's looking at the mess in the orchard.

"He did."

They walk among the trees, dodge several gallon-sized mounds of dung, apples and plums that don't look very digested. "Um," she says, looking at the big limbs ripped down, some still covered with apples. She points at the trunk of one, where the bark is ripped down to the ground, then at the tree next to them. "Why are the apples of that tree different colored?"

"They're different kinds. I've grafted them there."

"They don't get mixed up?"

"No, they stay true to the wood."

"Look at them all." She sees the tags, some flashing in the sun. "How many kinds?"

"Eighty or ninety kinds of apples, a dozen so plums, six kinds of pears. Some apricots. Just for fun."

She reads a tag, "Sixteen spy?"

"That's a cross I'm doing, a sweet-sixteen, which has a great flavor, with a northern spy that's a good keeper. Here, over here," he leads her, "the bear's left a few sixteens. Try this." He picks a ripe one, gold and orange.

She holds it, looks at it. "How do you do that? Cross them, I mean?"

"Pick out two of the best looking and get them a motel room."

She won't look at him, takes a bite of the apple.

"It's a long procedure," he repairs. "I put paper bags over the flower buds. When they open, I do the pollinating by hand, cross the ones I want, and then keep them covered until the petals drop. So bees don't mess them up. Then I tag them and hope for fruit. If I get any, I collect seeds from ripe fruit at the end of summer."

"Wow, this is good. What is it, vanilla? Licorice?"

"Great flavor, isn't it? This fruit's not my cross, but it carries the seeds of the mating. I plant them and hope they sprout. After another year or two, I cut wood from those seedlings and graft it on a good tree. Then I wait for them to grow fruit, and that will be the fruit of what I've joined."

"Must take forever."

"About that. I started five years ago, and I still haven't gotten an apple to try. Maybe next year. If bears don't tear them out."

She squeezes one eye shut. "Right. Isn't there anything you can do to keep him out?"

"I built a bear fence this summer. Around the orchard and all the buildings." He sweeps his arm. "Electrified. Got instruction from the beekeeper. Didn't you see it on the way in?"

"I did, but it was open." She gazes around. He points out a few places where the fence peeks in and out of all the understory. "It must have been a job down here cutting through all that briar and junk."

"Yep."

"So I don't get it." Her mouth is half parted.

"I was canning some plums last night, and I didn't get out to close the gate until just after dusk." He'd had extra syrup and decided to use it on a batch of pears he was drying, found himself so pleased and involved with this solution that he hadn't noticed how dark it was getting. "I've been leaving the gate open in the day, you know, to get mail and stuff. Never been a problem in the light of day."

She nods.

"So the bear had already slipped in, and I didn't see him. He got locked in all night."

"Oh." She claps her hand over her mouth, her eyes crinkling.

"Pretty goddamn funny, isn't it?" He tries to yawn, but quits when it proves fake.

"I'm sorry," she cries, laughs under her hand. "What are you going to do?"

"I don't know. What would you do?"

"He'll leave sometime, won't he?"

"Oh yeah, but probably not till after dark, and by then he'll be hungry enough to tear out what he didn't get last night."

"But you shot him. He's not going to hang around."

"I don't think you're thinking like a bear."

"You know how a bear thinks?"

"He's cramming on the pounds for winter fuel. In September he's one big eating disorder."

"You think he'll stay around long enough to tear it all up again?"

"I could pick all the apples left, but most of these are keepers, and they need another three or four weeks of growing, or they're no good. I could do that because I'd rather lose the crop than the trees."

"Can't you wait till he comes down, and then scare him away—I mean, if he doesn't leave on his own?"

"I bet he'll run right back up that tree."

"What if you get between him and that tree?"

"Might work, but I doubt that he'd let it happen. When he sees me."

"He won't come down till dark?"

"Probably not, or he would've done it by now."

She taps her fingers on the side of her leg. "You'd kill him if I weren't here?"

"I'd have me a rug and smoke some sausage."

"I don't believe you." She starts away. They walk out to the turnaround.

"Listen," he says, "I've been hearing it said the tribe's water crazy. A few neighbors warned me that the tribe's buying anything with water on it, river or creeks I mean, and that I'm a fool to be giving anything away, that it'll be hard enough, as it is, to hang on."

She cants her head. "It's no secret that the tribe's buying

ranches on rivers and creeks, ones that come up for sale. When we can do it, when we've got the money. And we'll take the conservation easements we can get. Why wouldn't we?" Her lips are thin and strict, barricaded. She hasn't said a thing about this land being theirs, treaty land before they got screwed out of it.

"Yeah," he says in a noncommittal way.

She leaves the subject. "So can I check back to see what your bear's doing?"

"If you'll stay for some dinner. You got family waiting?"

Her face stops where it is. Waiting same as him. She looks back toward the busted orchard. "No, I don't have family waiting. But I don't know about dinner."

"You come back to see what happens with this bum up the tree. There'll be something to eat if you're interested."

Toward evening the bear gets restless, climbs to the tip of the tree, and chews off cones, young gristly ones heavy as grenades. He makes chomping, popping sounds, and pieces filter down through the branches along with the green whisk-broom tips of branches. When he sees Johnny, he stops feeding, whoofs and breathes heavily. Johnny pulls up a lawn chair, slides down in it, so he can watch without straining his neck. The sky is gold and the top of the bear's tree is russet-red. Then Johnny hears the distant spit and pop of gravel, her vehicle coming down the hill. He walks out to meet her.

"He's still here?" she asks, slams the door of her old Chevy. The front is rusted, the headlights mounted in unpainted Bondo.

"Don't they give you a vehicle to use?"

"They do. But not today. Long story."

"I wouldn't let him leave till you got here. But I think he's getting restless. I could hear his stomach growling. Come on in first for some snacks."

"I don't want to miss him."

"No, we'll watch from a window. He won't come down with us out there anyway."

In the glassed-in back porch, Johnny has set up two wooden folding chairs, a card table with cheese and crackers. They have a view of most of the lower third of the tree, but the arborvitae on the corner of the well house hides the very bottom.

"Wine, beer, coffee, tea?" he asks.

She takes tea. He opens a beer. "All right. I'll have a beer, too," she says.

"With the tea?"

She's kneeling, craning her head to see up. "Hey," she says, "here he comes."

Johnny moves up alongside her, squats. The bear's backing down, his movements surprisingly certain and graceful. The animal stops halfway, peers around one side of the tree and then the other. Hatching a plan, Johnny guesses.

But the bear's waiting drags on. That's the thing about wild animals who don't read or listen to the radio, Johnny muses. Having whole days to while away, they can stand or sit or cling to the side of a tree and watch nothing forever. Johnny kneels, then gets down on his hands and knees. He has to be the furthest thing from a bear, can't seem to survive anywhere anymore without a chair.

Ramona's still in her original position. He decides to think about her. Maybe that's what bears and deer do, think about other bears, other deer. He remembers Ramona at the community meeting on closing the North Fork to whites. She said the mistake was that people got to thinking about that land up there as public land, but that it wasn't. It was Indian land, getting so much use that Indian families were finding it harder and harder to camp, hunt, fish, collect plants, do what they've always done up there because there were so many other people up there nowadays. She noted that a lot of the people in that room speaking out against the closing had "No Trespassing" or "Keep Out" signs on their own places.

But most of those folks didn't think it was the same, equating private land with tribal land, something about the collective that included them, too. Which was a strange way of thinking, to Johnny's mind.

When some of the folks from the university spoke, they didn't use the word Indian, which was interesting, because most of the tribe identified the term Native American with just those academics, this other set of invaders out to manifest more of somebody else's destiny. Like the New Agers who came later, the professors and grad students wanted to study tribal lives, publish books about ceremonies, healing plants, and other secrets that belonged to the tribe and nobody else.

These secrets, they were what tripped the white mind. When the tribe came up with a forest plan about how and where they would or wouldn't log, their guide and ideal became a forest resembling pre-Columbian forests that grew before fire suppression. Word got out somewhere that the tribe might have a model the Forest Service could learn from. But when National Public Radio wanted to send a reporter out, the tribe didn't want to talk about it. No doubt, the news agency considered the rebuff as sullen, or at least, inexcusably passive. By the tribe's reckoning, Johnny guessed, the silence was assertive. A sliver of sovereignty.

For Johnny, the conservation easement he wanted wasn't the donation of anything, because the rights they were supposedly negotiating weren't rights he ever really thought he owned, not on the rez. He didn't have to explain this to his puzzled white neighbors. His sliver of sovereignty maybe.

"It's getting pretty dark," Ramona says. "What are you going to do when we can't see him?"

"I don't know."

"Wait," she says. "Look, he's coming down. Ho, he's moving. There, he's gone. He went behind that tree."

Johnny is back on his hands and knees. "I'll watch this side of the well house. You watch over there to see if he goes toward the gate." He squints. "Damn, it got dark fast."

"I don't see him anywhere."

"Me neither."

They wait. Johnny imagines him tearing out grafts, ripping the bark down. That son of a bitch. "I'm going out," he says.

She's behind him at the door. Outside the gloom has filled in beneath the trees, under every lee. They creep around the well house. Johnny blinks, searches the orchard for some movement of dark black against lesser black.

They register each other at the same time. When the bear materializes, he's eating apples from a limb torn down the night before. He charges toward the big ponderosa he'd been in. Johnny races toward him and the tree, but the bear beats him, hurls his bulk up the trunk. He looks like a black Volkswagen driving into the sky. Ramona runs into Johnny. "Sheesh," he says. The bear's disappeared, but they can hear him breaking limbs and scraping the bark up above. "How can he do that?" Johnny says. "Run up a tree like that? He must weight three hundred pounds, and he just ran up it like there was no such thing as gravity."

"What are you going to do now?"

"Cut the tree down."

"You are not."

"Let's go eat. He's won't come down till three in the morning or something. What's he got to do? Where's he got to be? No-where. Everything he wants is here. The complete bear."

"Are there other bears that might come in?"

"I imagine. We could name them. You want to name them?"

"I want to know what you're going to do now."

"Pick everything?" he asks.

"In the dark?"

They go in. He's cooked a goose. He'd called Jasa, but she couldn't come out. She didn't say why, and he didn't tell her he had other company.

"This is really nice," Ramona says after they've been eating for a while. He appreciates her appreciating the meal, not saying much.

"Good," he says, and they go on eating. He passes potatoes and broccoli. Outside, a bear sits in the top of a tree. Apples dangle. Ramona hasn't asked any questions about Johnny's past, which means she's not up to inviting his probes. No bones, no ghosts, no airing. Leave them in their boxes.

"I don't think it'll work, picking all those apples in the dark," she says when they're at the sink with the dishes.

"Let's pick a bellyful," he says.

"A bear's belly?"

"He can only eat what will fit in him, but I'll pick them for him."

When they go out, she holds the light while he pulls down Lodi apples. They're soft, overripe apples, not the kind he favors anymore, and he's kept only one big limb of them. But it is a heavy bearer, and quickly, he fills the five-gallon bucket Ramona holds for him. They go to the base of the bear's ponderosa and dump them out in a pile.

"You think this'll work? You'll be able to sleep?" she asks.

"With one eye open."

"Can I call you in the morning?"

"Of course."

"Thanks for dinner." They're holding the beams of their flash-lights on each other's torso. She offers him her light.

"Any time. Let me walk you to your car."

At her car, she slams the door, mightily, three times before it latches, starts it up, and drives away. In the morning the bear is gone. The picked Lodi apples are gone, too. All that remain are the leaves and woody stems of some of the spurs Johnny broke off with the fruit.

He goes back in, makes coffee, sits on the porch in the sunlight, and waits for the phone to ring. He tries to imagine any people endangered by the presence of his twenty-year-old daughter, can't find any credibility until he admits that this girl intends a threat of her own. To be of any service, she has to be somebody's problem. He squeezes his eyes shut, finds himself back with the bear, marvels at the mechanics of bear delicacy, heretofore unknown, eating the apples but not the stems or leaves. This bulk of animal that can run up a tree as if it were a hill.

# ALL FALL DOWN

"I want you to miss her more," Maria told her father.

"Of course you do. We're like certificates for your existence. If we didn't make it as a couple, what does that say about your genes? You're a can of mismatched paint, that's what it says."

She laughed. "You don't think it works like that."

"Of course I don't. You're better than both of us added up. Nature knows what to do with mistakes like your mom and me. Nature wants to be proud, and she gets to be proud of you."

"Quit trying to talk-therapy me. I'm fine. Where are those boxes of Mom's stuff? There are things she wants."

"It's all on the back porch. Drive around back, and I'll help you load."

"Was it hard doing that? Going through everything?"

"I did it an hour a day. I can do anything an hour a day."

"I love the coping programs you assign yourself."

"The universe assigns, not me."

An hour after she left, he was in the kitchen at the sink when the tree came down. It was like an airliner had crashed into the house. Walls convulsed, glass busted. And it turned dark. He looked out the back porch windows, and it was as if a jungle had

71

sprung up. He tried to open the back door, but heavy, crooked limbs blocked it. He went through the house to the front door. In the living room, the ceiling was punched down. Nail-spiked butt ends of boards thrust down like wooden thunderbolts and blocked that door. He went upstairs, but he couldn't get far because the upstairs ceiling had bellied down. Hunching over, he made it to the closets where the wall there allowed him to half-stand. It was this wall that had punched the floor down along with the living-room ceiling below it. He went back downstairs and lunged at the back door until he got enough gap to squeeze through.

The big cottonwood couldn't have made a more direct hit. It diagonaled the house, nested its trunk into the cradle of the crushed roof. The tree's diameter in that traversing tapered from about four to two feet.

Rain was falling. He saw some picture frames under the splayed eaves, went over, and picked them up. They'd fallen from the upstairs bedroom. One was of Maria wading in the river as a girl. The other was of Irene standing in front of the Yellowstone Park Entrance (that one should go with her things). Nels looked up. The top log of the upstairs wall jutted out past the flattened roof. Fleeing the rain, he went to the wood shed and stood there with the two framed pictures and tried to take in the situation.

\*

If anything haunted him about the disintegration of their love, it was that he was not haunted enough about it. Puzzled, yes, terrifically. There was that morning they lay in bed together not touching, him conscious, her wherever she was when she slept like the dead, and he had this bizarre clarity. The notion was as absurd as the child's game, 'step on a crack, break your mother's back,' with the ridiculous provision that it was true, that he knew their dissolution was imminent and irreversible provided that she didn't touch him in the next hour or so, that she didn't smile at him or say anything affectionate. It was like changing the display settings on his computer, when it says if you don't finalize this change in the next 15 seconds, the settings will revert. So Irene didn't do anything any differently from any other morning, and their settings reverted. Just like that. One touch and it could've all been different.

Focusing a little tighter, he studied this notion. Like many of the axioms he'd begun to accumulate, it was true and it wasn't. It wasn't completely a could've-been-different kind of thing. Or pretty much not, he supposed. Yes, had she touched him, they still would've been married. But touching him wasn't what she was going to do. Thus, nursery-rhyme antics had to rescue them, make them do what they might not have ever gotten around to doing.

He went so far as to confront Irene about it. "So when were you going to bring it up?"

"I don't know," she said, and he believed her. By then, he knew what to believe about everything. Should the Fed change interest rates? He would've known if he cared.

In the settlement they agreed to, Irene got two-thirds of the land while he got the remaining third with the house. They averaged two appraisals on the house and after adjusting for the extra property she got, he owed her $40,000. Martin, his friend and colleague at the University, would loan him $20,000, which meant he had to come up with another $20,000 or sell the place. In town, Irene was buying a small house, and his cash settlement would be her down payment.

Nels was on the phone with Hal the insurance adjustor within an hour. The phone and power still worked. "You're not covered for falling trees, unless the tree fell during a storm," Hal told him.

"It was raining and windy. Is that a storm?"

"We didn't get any weather here in Armstead. I'll be out in the morning, and we'll look at it. What have you done to protect what's there now?"

"I've got a tarp in one spot, but the tree's blocking most of the roof. What's the definition of a storm?"

"Let me look at what we've got."

What we've got, Nels was thinking, is pretty straightforward. A tree on top of a house. That night he did not sleep well. He could almost touch the ceiling, and mosquitoes came in through all the holes and broken windows. Were there trees that just fell over on their own? Trees that would agree with any expert witness?

So now he was buying a broken house. Selling it wouldn't clear his debt, not without that insurance. But selling wasn't an option anyway. A broken house yes, but it was his broken house. He and the house were a suited pair. Bad luck did not account for this. You are a true loser, when nature goes out of her way to reveal it.

Up at first light, Nels had no breakfast. He made coffee but let it get cold. He stood outside and studied the lower half of the tree.

No weather in Armstead, the man said. The phrase sang in him like a Greek chorus. How many thousands of dollars depended on the definition of storm? What made a storm worth insuring against but not a giant, root-rotted cottonwood? The rain that came didn't hurt much of anything, but if it contributed to the definition of a storm, it was nothing but meaning.

He looked at the tree as if it were still falling, a dead weight of so much consequence. Then he went for the chain saw. In the woods behind the garage, Nels cut down and limbed two ponderosa poles fifteen feet or so in length and about as thick as the calf of his leg. By the time the adjustor had arrived, Nels had built a bipod support for the lower half of the tree leaning out over the front porch. The poles slanted toward each other butting into notches he cut into the belly of the fallen giant. He'd dug the lower ends of the poles into the ground so they wouldn't slip.

"That's pretty cool," the adjustor said, when he got out of his car. "You can cut that tree up without it sliding down and taking out your front porch."

"Yep," Nels said, "but that's not what's on my mind at the moment."

"That tree couldn't have found a way to do more damage." Hal shook his head.

"Yep, but that's not what's on my mind at the moment," Nels said.

"You're okay, Nels. We got a call from Carlyle for a place a mile or so from here. About a shed roof getting torn off. Like I said, we had nothing like a storm in Armstead, so it was just local."

"I'm covered?"

"You're covered."

"You want some coffee?"

"Would you have offered it if you hadn't been covered?"

"It wouldn't have been right if this tree slipped through the fine print."

"I'll have that coffee."

Nels mirowaved the coffee he'd intended for himself, while the adjustor went around the house, inside and out, upstairs and down, taking photos and notes. Hal finished his coffee while leaning on his car. "This is going to be a big project. It'll take a crane coming in, lifting off that roof to get logs back in place and then lowering it back to fix the rest. All those windows, two ceilings with the framing, the flooring, the chimney and roofing."

"There's a bridge over the spring where you drove in. I don't think you can get a crane across that."

"We'll have to buttress up that bridge."

"What kind of money are you talking about, Hal?"

"I don't know. I'm guessing forty thousand, somewhere in there."

"What if I did it?"

"Really? How would you do it? With a crew? A crane?"

"I don't know. However I could do it."

"I'll get back to you on that, Nels."

"Who's going to decide?"

"There are four of us who will go over it all."

"What are my chances?"

"Have you got any experience in this kind of work?"

"It's my house, Hal. And I'm good with messes."

Martin and five other guys from the Carlyle Volunteer Fire Department showed up a half hour after the adjustor left. In minutes, they had three chain saws running. On the roof, two of them lugged limbs and trunk segments to the thrust-out eaves where they dropped them to the ground. The wood was heavy, dripping wet wood, and it was all two men could handle to drop a two-foot stump off the roof without it getting away from them and making more mischief. On the lawn, two others dragged and rolled the pieces of tree into the woods. It took all day.

Nels called Maria in Armstead and asked her to bring out several cases of beer when she came. She brought two pizzas, as well. Martin raked leaves, sticks, and shakes out of the way for an opening on the front lawn. They righted a group of stumps there for stools, sat, drank, ate, and joked into the twilight. Nels looked off over the heads at the naked collapse of his roof. Both gables still stood even though the windows there were broken out.

They wanted to know his plan of action, assuming he got the job. He didn't have one yet. He didn't want to plan anything until he knew he could. Even as he denied this, he knew there was a root cellar in his brain, where there was probably some figuring going on he didn't have access to yet.

"I have two house jacks you can use," Daryl said.

"Thanks, Daryl. I'll get them right away. If it's a go."

"I've got a hand-winch and a come-along," Larry said, "and two truck jacks, hydraulic, those little squat guys."

"Thanks. We'll see."

Hank had a come-along and a fence stretcher.

"How the hell's he going to make use of a fence stretcher?"

"I'll take them both," Nels said. "Stretch sounds like something I'll be needing to do."

The next day, Hal called. "They'll let you do it for thirty."

"I swear you said forty."

"Yeah, the other guys thought it could be done for less."

"No, they didn't. They knew I'd agree to less."

"Maybe. You going to take it?"

"Thirty five."

"Thirty firm, Nels. You know I can have my crew in there in a week. Put you up in a hotel. Have you back home by the Fourth of July."

Silence.

"Nels?"

"So Dad, do you have any advice?" Maria and her fiancé, William, were planning a September marriage.

"I'm the wrong person to ask. Unless you're wanting to know what to do that we didn't."

"I guess. Or not to do."

She was trying to avoid making him feel like a failure, he guessed, but the question intrigued him. "Is there anybody out there you don't like?"

"What?"

"Anybody you hate? Let me ask you what you could have done to keep from hating them?"

"I'm talking about the person you live with, the one you marry."

"I'm talking about the person you don't like, how you or that other person let it happen. There's a program involved. Tell me how much you understand it, what you could've done to steer it in a different direction."

"When I don't like somebody, it has to do with values that aren't the same, about respect that you don't have to start with."

"Not liking somebody starts from zero somewhere. And then you make it not work, the not-liking-them part, and so do they." He stopped to puzzle this. What did he really think about his daughter's chances? Was it honest in trusting they had a better chance than he and Irene had? Lots of pros and cons, this looking at everything straight on. And by that he meant straight straight-on, not a little bit crooked straight-on. Any hedging, any provisions were as bad as using coefficients in experiments, sponges for sopping up whatever you couldn't account for.

"So you and Mom worked at not liking each other."

"Kind of. You won't want to think of us as children, but that's what it is, the crybaby who isn't sure just how much he or she is getting mistreated. Imagine the child in me thinking she doesn't love me anymore. She did once, but she must not have known me or pretended to, because now after thirty years, she looks in the bucket and it's full of nothing but disappointment. So then of course, that makes me disappointed, too, having to live with this person, once love this person, who ultimately calls me out and accuses me of fooling her, of bamboozling her decades ago into believing I was somebody she could love. Couldn't be simpler, just that fast, two bad seeds planted. She scammed me, I could say, and then of course, as an accuser I have scammed her, and there we are—two little babies with bitter, broken hearts." He stopped. He'd overstated it. He was always doing this. Drama has an agenda of its own. "Wait," he said. He scratched, both hands behind his ears.

"I...I...thought you'd grown apart or something," she groped. "You make it sound like treason. Or something satanic."

"No, you're right, let me get my hand off the scale," he said. "I said babies, children, and I mean that. You know, if Irene suddenly decided after a year or two—she won't, of course—that she made a mistake, that she still had feelings for me, it would cancel out all my bitterness, all my anger. I think it could do that. How stupid is that? See. What could be more childish? There's all this blind, furious passion but it's based on plucking petals from a daisy. And right now, 'she loves me not.'"

"Oh, Dad, I can't believe that. You can't make it such a silly little thing. Not something that old. With all that investment? And me? Just wave it all away. I mean, look what it's done to your lives. You're both alone. It couldn't be sadder."

"I know. I wonder what you'll tell your children."

"When we get divorced, you mean?" She looked stricken.

"No after thirty years of learning about each other."

"Is that it? You just bleed out all the surprises. In the great gray emptiness of familiarity?"

"No, that's not it either, no dripping water wearing down rock till it's gone. Maybe it's got to do with what you expect of love, and if you make the other person that emblem of love, they end up taking the fall when love ages, when you lose strands of it like your hair. Maybe that's why I could imagine loving your mom again, if she loved me. But I have to say it would be knowing it would be a different kind of love, one that's on sale. Like day-old bread, you know, not fresh and warm, but not that bad either. Something you could live on well enough."

"Do you suppose it's possible to think about these things too much?"

"I don't know how to choose what I think about. Do you?"

"I thought I did."

He nodded.

"But you don't?"

"What do I know, Maria? Even if I complain about the little kid I am, I'd still rather be that than believe I can be an adult and make wise grown-up decisions that will work out for the best in the end."

Maria bent her head and pinched the bridge of her nose.

"What?"

"I don't know what to think if people don't get wiser when they age."

"They get wiser at hiding from what they don't know."

"Well, that's something isn't it? Something you know more about than I do. Isn't that what wisdom's all about?"

"We're always hoping for better, aren't we? It's an old DNA trick."

"I think it's better when you're not sad."

"That's called circular reasoning."

"I don't care. I still think it's better when you're not sad."


Nels made a sixteen-foot beam by nailing three two-by-sixes together. On one end, he bolted one of the house jacks. He butted the jack-end of the beam under a sprung log and then, standing on a ladder, he pumped the jack handle until he had tension to keep it in place. Down the ladder he went and up the stairs into the bedroom. He stretched a come-along across the room from the sprung log to the corresponding but intact log on the opposite side. When he took in the slack, the cable stretched over the bed, a guitar string just over Irene's pillow. Down the stairs he went, up the ladder. He jacked the end of the log in about a foot.

He warmed up the quarter cup of coffee left and, then sipping, sat on a stump underneath that wall and studied it. A little later, he built a second beam mounted with another jack. This one he butted under the roof plate above the sprung log. When he cranked that plate up, the roof creaked as if in pain. He moved the ladder back and forth between the two jacks, pumping each handle a little. Upstairs, he took the slack on the come-along. Downstairs, then up the ladder again. By late afternoon he had the log back in place. Still, he dared not release the come-along. The weight of the splayed roof rafters and sheeting would probably shove the plate and the log out again. He was going to be stepping over the cable and sleeping under it for a time. Nevertheless, the wall looked intact, and he hadn't spent a cent yet.

When Maria came out that evening, he wanted to show her what he'd done. "And I think I have a plan for the front room ceiling and the upstairs floor." Don't brag, he told himself. "Where I won't have to take it all that apart," he went on.

"I thought those ceiling boards inside were broken."

"Yep. The joists. They are." He waited for her to want to know more.

"I'm glad to see you doing this. Figuring this out."

"Huh?"

"I can tell you feel better about everything. Mechanical dilemmas are therapy for the male mind."

"I'm just trying to get mosquitoes out of the bedroom. Did I tell you the insurance people were talking about rebuilding the bridge to bring in a crane? I haven't spent anything yet." Still crowing, he was.

"So why wouldn't they do it your way?"

"My way is going to take most of the summer and a lot of

coffee. They were going to throw forty thousand at it and have it done in ten days or two weeks. What's Irene saying about all this?"

"That it was good she was in charge of getting good home insurance."

He tried to keep from frowning.

"What?"

Nothing." He stared at the ground. How vast this distance between him and his once-upon-a-time wife. Looking back, it seemed not that long ago he and Irene had put their hearts in separate witness-protection programs. All under this tree-broken roof.

"I'm sorry," Maria said.

"Nothing to be sorry about. Look, I'm dying to tell you how I aim to fix those joists without touching them."

"Tell me," she said, but her enthusiasm was fake. She was being a good sport.

He threw up his hands. "I'm sorry. Why should that interest you?"

"It does, Dad. Tell me."

He shook his head, then picked up a stray limb and flung it. "How was your mother about this? Did it make her sad? I mean, this was the house she lived in, too. Was it…" he trailed off.

"Of course. I suppose, but she didn't say anything about being sad."

He nodded, thinking he already knew that.

About a five-foot section of the brick chimney had got knocked off. It left a crater in the roof before it toppled over the edge, went down on the lawn, and gouged out a huge slab of sod. How was he going to get that back up? And then there was the question of the wiring. He'd left the light circuit on upstairs but not the receptacles. He should ask an electrician whether continuity in the circuit implied the insulation on the wire and all the connections would be intact. No, of course it wouldn't imply that.

Deal with the problem at hand, he told himself. Keep moving. In the living room, he used a shorter rig with a mounted jack and pushed the ceiling up enough to open the front door. He cranked on the jack in intervals of every few hours or so to give the ceiling time to unbend. The next day he worked upstairs, and in a similar manner, jacked up the roof ridge until the broken framing and sheeting would yield no more. He rebuilt the two small closets facing each other across a short hallway. The bottom plates of these he anchored with long bolts through the floor, past the broken joists, to the front-room ceiling beneath.

He would wait for a forecast of clear, rainless weather for a few days before making his next move, this one where he would tear off the shakes, the roofing, the broken rafters and replace everything. With one addition. The new rafters over the closet he would double up, nail two together to replace the single broken ones. Once he had the roof weatherproofed, he would return to the bedroom and extend the closet walls up to these reinforced rafters. Anchored from above, those walls bolted to the broken joists below (and unseen) would hold the floor and ceiling beneath just fine.

No contractor would ever leave a broken infrastructure like between the two floors. But they wouldn't be paying for it either, a neatness cost they would simply pass onto the owner. What any adult would do. The lesson for Nels of course was the same for any mess. It was what you did with your head that mattered in the end.

That weekend, Maria came out. "Mom wants to see the house if it's all right with you."

"Why wouldn't it be all right with me?"

"She doesn't want to upset you."

"Really?"

"Yes, really."

"I could say that, too, couldn't I? That I wouldn't want to upset her."

"What are you getting at?"

"I wouldn't have to say that, because I don't think there's anything I could do to upset her."

"Of course there is."

"No, I mean, that's plausible."

"Don't be weird about this."

"For her, I am a rock or a stick, something inert. For me, she is an unstable compound, potentially volatile. I can be harmed, not her."

"You're pushing it."

"Your mother settles with people, with events. You know how it is if something really bad or really good happens, it takes a while to adjust. Your mother adjusts in a nanosecond. Maybe I never entirely get that job done."

"What shall I tell her? She'll understand."

"That's what I'm saying. But tell her to come look at it. I'll deal with it. I'll think of it as an exercise, what you would call a coping program."

Maria smirked. "I'm not talking about this anymore."

The rest of that week plagued him. Instead of his deliberate thoughtful approach, he found himself pushing to accomplish. He wanted the chimney up, windows back in the gables. Stupidly, he tried to come-along the chimney up a makeshift ramp made out of two of the new two-by-sixes he'd bought to replace rafters. When one of the planks slipped, the other broke, and the chimney went down and gouged out more lawn.

The next day was a Friday, and Maria called in the morning to tell him Irene had decided not to come.

"Why?" His voice was angry.

"She said she just didn't think it was a good idea."

"Did you tell her it wasn't a good idea?"

"Noooo," she cried. "Dad…"

"I'm sorry, Maria. I've got to go." He would've lied about what he had to go do, but he hadn't time to think of anything. He hung up and went outside. He sat on the chimney's brick corpse for a while. Then he went back, rustled through his brand-new divorce folder, found Irene's phone number, and called her.

"Nels," she said, her voice bright with surprise.

"Yeah, I'm not sure why I'm calling, Irene. I…I'm not sure what to think anymore."

"I know this is hard for you, Nels. But it'll get better, a lot better. It won't be long, and you'll be happier than you've been in a long time. Please believe that."

"Sounds like you've been divorced a long time. In your own mind, I mean."

"I have. I think it's important we don't consider this like it's anybody's fault."

"I don't know how to think like that."

"That may be true but know it's true on my part. If that helps. I'm really sorry about the house. Maria thinks it may be helping though, the work you're doing."

"The house. You don't think of it as our house."

"Not now. I have to move on, Nels. I have my own demons."

"Have I ever met those demons? Do I know any of them by name, I mean?"

"You know them. But we don't want their names. We don't even want to talk about them, Nels, not anymore. You do understand that, don't you?"

"I don't know that I do."

"I'm going to go now, Nels. Be strong. Be glad you have Maria. That's what I'm doing."

As he paused to answer, she hung up. Her sudden absence startled him. He groped to remember what he was going to say, but he'd lost it. He sucked air through his teeth. It was almost unendurable, not knowing, not ever remembering what he was going to say.

# THE CAROLINA WREN

"Cantrell," she calls and stampedes through the back door into the kitchen. "There's a bird out there I've never heard before. Come listen. Hurry."

He rises slowly from his chair at the table, obedient but recalcitrant. "Here? Never heard it here before?" It's the end of March. "Never heard it anywhere. Hurry up."

They stand out in the afternoon sun, stare off into the rose bramble beneath river-bottom cottonwoods and listen. As warm as the light is, he can feel the chill of frost hanging in the shadows waiting to leak out again if a cloud covers the sun. Then the bird sings. Cantrell is amazed, first by the bold power of the song's pure notes and then by his own surprise. She is always making him look, listen, or smell something when, wish as he might, whatever she showcases never delights him as much as it does her. But he knows at once, if he'd heard this bird first, he'd have gone in and fetched her. "What the hell is it?" he asks. They can't see it. The song emerges from a taller tangle of rose, clematis, and chokecherry.

"It's not a mockingbird, but it has that same strong, ringing call."

He's never heard a mockingbird. Mockingbirds don't live in the northern Rockies. She has her binoculars up and is crouched and pivoting, searching as if on infantry patrol. "The bastard," she whispers, "he's hiding."

When the bird sings again, Cantrell is freshly surprised. It's like an opera singer has come to visit a neighborhood hither-to home to folk singers only. Swiftly, he's aggravated by its pre-eminence and distracting mystery. He and Rainy have been quar-reling, and here comes some goddamn bird to weaken the isolation of a good sulk.

It's not the usual fight. This time, Rainy has the cops look-ing for her. If anybody recognized her from the photo in the pa-per, Sheriff Lockner would be coming to their door and carting her off. They'd have some god-awful legal bills, some kind of fine maybe, and she'd be stuck in the slammer for what? A month, six months? It won't be some little slap on the wrist, not when the court has to think about deterring others from believing they could shape state politics by assault, in this case by breaking in on the governor and pouring used motor oil all over his desk and his lap. Rainy was wearing a Lone Ranger outfit, but a photographer caught her in the parking lot pulling off her mask. So far, they haven't identified her.

Three days before, when Cantrell was in Armstead, he saw her behind the Plexiglas of every newspaper vending box, a grainy profile of his wife stripping off her mask. At the moment, he tried on the idea that all he really wanted was a brand new courage, the capability, the power to live without her. They weren't suited. They weren't even close to being suited. Their fights were more frequent and more vehement.

"Do you have to go to every goddamn nature-crisis meeting in the northwest? I mean what would happen to all of nature if you missed one?"

She leaned at him from the waist. "Why do you say things like that? We met at the Three Rivers auction. There you were. What the hell were you doing there?"

"I was looking for you."

"That's not true, but even if it were, are we all that matters now? Just us. Screw the world. Leave it to corporate America?"

"There are limits. You have to believe in limits. If three migrant workers met in Seattle to protest some timber sale in the Gobi Desert, you'd drive through the night to get there."

"You knew who I was, Cantrell. If you're this surprised after thirteen years, whose fault is that?"

"Most folks mellow out a little, Rainy. I mean, after a while don't you get to live a little? Don't you get tired of galloping off to fight Shell Oil and the WTO? Can't you see the futility of going up against these armies of vampires? There you are, flailing at the universe. I don't have a lot of respect for that anymore. After a point, it's just stupid."

"I do live a little, Cantrell. I live a lot." Her mouth pursed the way it did when all restraint went over the dam. "I don't sit here self-satisfied looking at the world like it's all beneath me, all the lemmings getting what they deserve. You're smug, Cantrell. And a baby. What's to respect about that?"

A baby? Where did that come from? He only wonders this every other hour or so.

The bird doesn't sing again, and he goes back in. From the back porch he watches Rainy on this new-bird patrol, oblivious to his absence.

At the Three Rivers Resource Council Dinner and Auction thirteen, almost fourteen, years before, Rainy sat across the table from him. He liked her looks, so what? He'd learned years ago that, no matter how instinctual, physical attractiveness was not a reliable indicator of anything workable and was, in fact, an alert for danger. But it was her pleasure, her spirited involvement in the auction that kept his fix upon her. She was having a good time and saying things that made him laugh. Maybe she saw him watching, because she turned to him.

"Are you a rancher, Mr. Cantrell?" She'd thrust her face to read his name tag.

"What's the tell? I'm not wearing anything western, no more than your average schoolteacher or lawyer these days."

"You show the weather."

"That's more my age than the weather," he returned.

"Nope. You've got no more than ten years on me. Let me see that two-tone neck. Pull your collar back a little." She pulled her own back as a guide.

He shrugged, hooked his forefinger in his shirt and tee-shirt and gave her a peek. When she smiled triumph, he glanced down at the exposed wedge at the top of his chest. Sidewall white.

"Do your neighbors know you come to these Commie functions?" she probed.

"One of them does, the one who got me signed up. He's here somewhere."

"You're worried about what might happen to your ground water. Is that what's got you worried?"

"Not me. I'll be retiring in another five or ten years anyway. I'm only here because I'm a pure idealist."

"Yeah, but some of your neighbors are taking checks from Peabody and Rio Tinto. You know what those energy companies will do. Tell me that's got nothing to do with it."

"If it isn't all self-interest, what brings you here?"

"I'm the idealist. I've got to be here to sleep nights."

He should've believed her. Instead he went on with their play. "You owe it to your kids, right?"

"I don't have kids, only dogs. How about you?"

"No kids."

She hesitated at this. "Maybe you are an idealist then. Or is it for the land perhaps, the land all by itself?" She sharpened an increment, her mouth partly open, tentative, her eyes…well, he wasn't intending to believe any of it, but there they were, those eyes inviting him to think of her any way he wanted to. Just like that, there was lust afoot, and they both knew it. That was his second warning. Attractive and she knew what was what, while he didn't know much more than what wasn't. He was out of her class, and market, too, one he hadn't been in for years.

But there was more than one Cantrell there that night, one of them sharp enough to know what was happening before it did, and the other who didn't care, reckless and stupid enough to bid on her donation. A hundred bucks to TRRC and she'd host a picnic in Red Lantern State Park, one replete with BLT's and brie, edamame beans, pomegranate cheesecake, and homemade wine. It sounded like a rendezvous on the flanks of Mount Olympus. At play among the mountain sprites.

Three weeks later, they sat in cottonwood shade, and she was pouring that fruit wine in little pottery cups. "Rainy," he asked, "that's not the name your parents gave you?" A neutral question, he'd prefigured. He didn't want things moving too fast.

"Would you ever think of me as a Catherine?"

"I still don't know who to think of you as."

"But you would like to know me better?"

"Are you flirting with this old man?"

"You have to be the oldest man on the earth if you have to ask that."

A shudder made him lurch.

"What?" she cried.

"I could get awful used to being around you." He shielded both eyes with one hand and looked at the ground.

"I could get used to being around you, I think. Why are you taking this like a death in the family?"

"I don't have anything like you in my itinerary." He lowered his hand and looked at her again.

"Why would you have anything like an itinerary? That sounds like a dumb thing to do."

"Or smart, depending on your point of view."

"Oh Cantrell, it's time to live a little."

"I was afraid you'd say something like that."

When she comes back in, she goes to her computer and googles bird songs. An hour of that, and she comes back into the kitchen and stands at the sink facing away from him. "I can't find him," she says.

"I'm not talking to you," he says. "If I knew you, I'd be an accessory to the crime."

"Crime?" She turns. "What I did is no real crime. Not in the scale of things."

"I'm not going to talk to you about this. You're grounded now. You'll have to think of this like house arrest. What did you do with your costume?"

She opens the refrigerator door. "What do you want for dinner, Cantrell? Carbonara or enchiladas?"

At breakfast, he's contrite, but he doesn't want to let on. Yes, he is a baby. He aches to have her sit down and have coffee and toast with him, to read a magazine article and say nothing at all. Instead she's on her cell phone pacing. Their odd estrangement wounds to such an extent he's back to wondering if he'd be happier alone. This is a drill he makes himself suffer. Could he survive her absence? How could they be so different, so aggravated by each other, and so fucking dependent at the same time? Why would it be completely out of the question for him to slip back to his good, stolid, weather-measured existence? Why does any existence seem so colorless and death-shadowed without her light, even when it includes the battles, her endless diversions?

This is a pain he never expected, so exquisitely searing that at times he can feel the pull, the sweet solace of simply being dead. It was like everything mattered too much anymore, and he had neither the intensity nor the faith to man the barricades nor the courage of equanimity to watch her inflamed dedication. A woman avowed. What he had instead was this new fear and incapability of being alone. How had this once gritty Cantrell come to be a sad sack? If she'd enriched his life, she'd eviscerated him, too, opened him like a surgeon would, only her cutting and sawing was done carelessly, not willfully or intentionally careless but in passing, trusting of course that everyone was as oblivious as she. How could anyone live with so little sense of consequence? She was the arrow waiting to be notched on the bowstring and then aimed at the sky or the ocean or abyss or who knows fucking where. Twang.

Earlier that morning she'd heard the bird again and caught a glimpse of it. "It's a wren," she told him, her face twisted with disbelief. "He's not even half the size of what he sounds like." She went through the bird book and then back to the computer to call up wren songs. After a half hour of that, she sat slumped and flummoxed. She went back to the bird book. He heard her murmuring "Has to be, has to be." Again, she went to the computer.

He was grateful she had a project at home. "Getting it narrowed down?" he called to her.

"Umm," she said, terrifically distracted, "this one has different songs. The only one it . . ." she trailed off.

"Can be," he said. "Can be," he whispered.

But she wasn't listening, her presence like water about to boil. Then she stood and her chair fell back whack-clattering on the fir floor. "I got him," she was pointing, her arm long as Moses's. "That's him."

Cantrell listened to the recording. It was him. *Would-you-would-you-would-you* in barreling purity.

"A Carolina wren," she murmured.

He goes back to his breakfast alone as usual, but this time she's on her cell with somebody in the Zoology Department at the U in Armstead. Better them than her usual rabble.

"Really?" she says, her tone suddenly arrested. He glances over his shoulder. Her eyes look like garage doors going up. He's uneasy, but he doesn't know why.

"I understand that," she responds, "but I know it is. Bewick's? It's not Bewick's. Bewick's doesn't have a song like this. What? No. No. Yes, yes, I can. Give me your email address. I will. Yes, I will. I will." She's scribbling.

Yes, she will, Cantrell says to himself. Sometimes, she can say or do something that swamps him with desire. And right now, the quick way she says 'I will' three times accomplishes it. He imagines them grappling, how when she comes, it's like she's landing a big fish. He blinks and sucks a little packet of air through his teeth.

She hangs up and marches over to front him.

"Sit down," he says, "and tell me."

"You won't believe this."

"No, and I won't listen unless you sit down."

"They don't believe me."

"Sit down, Rainy."

She starts to sit. "That bird is a Carolina wren . . ." She's stopped halfway, Z-shaped, radiant. He imagines her bracing against the fish. He imagines her as the fish. He's always awed, maybe a little diminished, by the crescendo that overtakes her. "Sit, sit, sit," he demands.

She does.

"Good dog, Rainy."

"That bird has been never recorded in the state. They don't

believe me, because it would be a state record, and because it's...
what?...something like a thousand miles from its range. They
think it's a Bewick's."

"What's a Bewick's?" He pushes toast and coffee at her. "Eat,
drink."

"Another kind of wren. I've got to get a photo." And then
she's up and gone.

He closes his mouth and listens. Upstairs, then down, and out
the door, Rainy and her camera. Watch out, wren. Cantrell eats
her toast.

One of Russell Lockner's deputies arrests her the next morning. Somebody in Heron County, no doubt, finally got around to
their paper, recognized her, knew she'd be the one to do it, and
then squealed on her. They hold her most of the day while Cantrell
arranges to put the ranch up for her bond. When Lockner sees
him in the courthouse hallway, he cants his head, lifts his open
hand and shoulders. "I know, Russell," Cantrell says. "You had no
choice."

"Jesus H, Cantrell. She could of yelled in his face or something," the sheriff said. "She went way too far."

"I know," Cantrell says again.

It's quiet in the car on the way home until she asks if he's
heard the wren. He doesn't answer her question. At length, he
says, "I've talked to Harold Newburg, and he'll represent you."

"You didn't need to do that. I'm going to plead guilty. I thought
about all this before I did it."

"What are you going to do in jail if they stick you there for
three months? Or six? Harold said it's possible since it's your second offense."

"I'm going to read *War and Peace* and *Ulysses* and some of
those other big bastards I've always wanted to read. While I'm do-

ing yoga. Maybe I'll learn Spanish so I can talk to the fruit pickers in Henderson."

"You got yourself all figured out, don't you? I'm trying to understand where I fit into this, he-who-puts-up-bail."

"I'm sorry, Cantrell." Her head falls. "I know you didn't sign up for any of this, and now you'll have a wife in jail. It was a very selfish thing to do. But I got myself in a corner. Before he was governor, Mitchell said he would not let that pipeline cross those refuges. He told the League that pointblank. I was there and the sonofabitch said that." Her voice lifts. Then she stops. "He doesn't get to do that without any repercussions," she trails away.

When silence prevails again, she broaches it gently. "Did you hear the wren this morning?"

"When I went out to the barn."

"Did you see him?"

"I didn't look for him, Rainy. But he was pretty close to the house."

"That means I can get a picture of him. I know I can."

"Before you go to jail."

"Before I go to jail."

Rainy stalks the wren for three days before she finally gets a blurry shot of him in the shadows. "You can see the markings," she says and points at the monitor, at a fuzzy blob with no markings whatsoever that Cantrell can make out. When Rainy wants something bad, her brain fills in for what her eyes miss. She emails the photo to Professor Altimus and waits. Rainy checks her email three or four times an hour but doesn't hear back until the next day. Altimus writes back that the quality of the photo is too poor. He argues for the likelihood of it being another wren—canyon, marsh, house, but especially Bewick's—and then relates how difficult it had been for him a year ago to identify a marsh wren. Rainy snatches up her camera and heads for the brush.

For the next four or five days, she sends off a progression of photos, all with the same result that the quality is too poor for an identification. Moreover, what she's sent isn't enough to persuade a visit by anyone in the department. When it occurs to Rainy that it was the song that identified him, she resolves to get a recording. Her digital camera has a small recording device for taking notes on particular photos. Two more days of stealth and patience, and she captures a few fragments of the song on this tiny camera recorder. She emails the photos with the soundtrack intervals attached.

Cantrell sees the reply she gets the next day:

> *The sound info did not come along with the pictures, so I suspect that it is specific to the software of your camera. Does it save the sound as a .wav file or something else that you can send along? But a good photo would get a verdict.*
>
> Bernard Altimus

"Damn," Rainy says. "He's a wren. He doesn't sit still. He likes dark, brushy places. What's a .wav file?"

"You didn't ask me that?"

She doesn't answer. She's consulting her computer, fount for every technical conundrum.

"How will you live without that computer?"

"What?"

"In jail."

She's not listening. The computer, this other mate of hers, is telling her what a .wav file is. Murmuring, squirming, she wrestles with that challenge for an hour or so. That afternoon, she gets her best photo of the wren and sends it with her recordings, freshly rendered (she believes) in the required .wav format. While Cantrell marvels that she can use that machine to make what she wants, what perplexes him most is how she came to believe she could do it. It's a sort of certainty he regards alternately as admirable, absurd, and arrogant. An effrontery a baby like him finds hard to suffer.

The next morning he hears her yelling downstairs. Images flutter out: cows in the garden, a tree fallen in the yard, a bear on the porch, fire in the kitchen. He lumbers down the stairs. He's still threading his belt, aiming to protect them with his resolve, with iron detachment.

She's standing at the computer. "They believed me," she wails. "Look, and here's another letter already. It's true. It's official. The first Carolina wren ever recorded in the state."

Skeptical, he reads the notification:

*Congratulations. Your recordings confirm the first record of this species in the state. I am informing the State Birds Record Committee of this discovery. You should hear from them directly. This is really exciting. Good job.*

*Bernard Altimus*

Cantrell swallows. Why is it, he wonders, that everything he believes about her, he also disbelieves. "What do you know," is all he manages to say.

She clicks open the second letter:

*My name is Casey Daniel, and I am the current chairman of the State Bird Records Committee. I must alert you that there is a large birding public out there today and they are all connected on the web. The interest in your discovery will be very high (to say the least) when this gets out. How do you feel about visitors? Is there a way that they might see the bird without invading your privacy? I won't post this news until I hear from you. What an incredible find!*

*Casey.*

"Oh Jesus," Cantrell says.

"What?"

"So I'm here running Disneyland for you, while you sit in jail reading fat books about Russian wars."

She laughs that free way of hers, head tipped back, tongue pressed down making a dark hollow behind her teeth. She isn't even listening. "This is such great fun." When she looks at him again, she sobers a little. "Lighten up, Cantrell. The trial isn't for three weeks. That wren could leave tomorrow."

Gracious Rainy writes back that all are welcome. In a mere thirty minutes, the phone rings. A birder seventy miles south is on his way. Could he get directions?

"What have you done?" Cantrell asks her.

She writes directions to Casey Daniel and tells them where they can park on the hill.

Cantrell says: "I'm going to tell them all you're going to jail. You break laws and assault governors."

"They don't care where I'm going, Cantrell. These are fanatics, and all they care about is this bird. And like I said, that wren could leave tomorrow."

But the wren doesn't leave tomorrow or the day after. Or the week after, or the month. He's there every morning, and it's his song that wakes them at seven thirty in March, rising earlier with the sun in April, belting out his first punchy refrains at six thirty. The robins, ever noisy in the growing light, seem to quiet a little, and listen on to the putative grandeur of this tiny invader. This lost idiot, their puzzled hush seems to say. Who is this guy anyway?

The birder who arrives that first day reminds Cantrell of a retired detective or FBI agent. Old but alert, a little reticent, his Nordic blue eyes wandering about collecting, tall and silver-haired, calculating as a poker player always on that ridge between folding or betting. He's standing in front of their porch. "I haven't heard him for a couple of hours," Rainy says, her tone apologetic.

"I've got a recorder with speakers," the agent says absently, his gaze kiting about.

"You mean with the song of a Carolina wren?"

He nods.

"And that will bring him in or make him sing?"

"A decent chance."

"Do it then," Rainy blurts. "I want to see this."

"Only problem is," and this time he looks at Cantrell, in the mistaken belief perhaps that Cantrell wears the pants here, "if it's a young male, it could scare him off."

"Oh. No." Rainy stiffens. "Then you can't. Nobody else has seen him. We won't take any chance on that."

"No, you're right. Out of the question at this point. Where was he hanging out last?"

"At any point," Rainy says (as in MY Carolina wren). "Come, I'll show you."

Cantrell watches them cross the lawn. Now what? he's wondering. I can't mow or fix the coop roof or make any other disturbance now that this all belongs to the wren?

The agent gets a glimpse, and it chokes him up, Rainy attests. The next morning at first light, the agent's back, but there are a half dozen other birders in the yard as well. Rainy, in her robe, goes out to meet them. Cantrell watches from the window. They are all men burdened with binoculars, spotting scopes, cameras, and tripods, their distracted heads flitting here and there while they talk to Rainy, who in her white robe gesticulates like an angelic choir director. There in the kitchen, Cantrell hears the wren call. He watches, mesmerized, at the troops galvanized, leaning into the wind of that call, swoop off through the predawn gloom toward the raspberry patch, the white tails of Rainy's robe and the spindly legs of tripods flying after. Cantrell turns the coffee water off and goes out the back door to follow them. He stands behind to watch this huddle of hushed, thrilled whispers, pointing arms, all of them leaning out from the waist, barreled lenses shooting from their faces. When the wren moves, they shift in synchrony like a dance troop. Safely, Cantrell could pick every pocket.

Later, when Rainy comes in, he puts her coffee cup in her hand and makes her sit and tell him about it. As Rainy recounts her blow-by-blow, clots of birders pass in twos or threes by the kitchen window, catching the corner of his left eye, and by the front window, catching the right.

"Three of them drove from the other side of the divide. Do you know that two of them out there have already seen Carolina wrens."

"I thought you said—"

"One in Georgia, the other in Louisiana. And listen to this, you can hear Carolina wrens when you're watching the Masters Golf Tournament on TV. In fact, they were considered so much a part of that tournament that they actually set up recordings of them with speakers in the trees. Until they got flak for faking the ambience."

"Do we still get to live here, mow the lawn and stuff?"

She was looking at him but her eyes went somewhere else. Then she returned. "They have to mow the golf course."

"Thank you."

On cloudy days, the wren is often quiet. Some birders who have driven a long way will wait for hours, and Rainy takes out lawn chairs and positions them facing the vine and bramble heaps the wren frequents most often. One couple drives from the west coast through three states for no other purpose but to see this wren. They drive through the night and arrive at dawn. When they open their car door, they haven't gotten both feet on the ground before the wren blasts away. While they pursue him through the brush for a photo, Rainy cooks Cantrell's favorite breakfast for the four of them: soft-boiled eggs in a cup with salt, pepper, Tabasco, and butter; two slices of toast; and steamed baby turnips and greens. A week later, the couple sends copies of their wren photos and a book on bird behavior.

Rainy posts one of those photos on the fridge, and Cantrell stops now and then to speculate upon it. This tiny bird, his thin and quite finely shaped beak wide open thrust at the sky, his tail—a kind of little shingle stuck there—also straight up suffuses the bird with a wren-that-roared certainty and ferocity. Brick red on top and pale lemon beneath, he has a white racing stripe through his eye. Carolina? Georgia? What in God's name is he doing here way out west? If he's singing for a mate, as Rainy says, it's like Robinson Crusoe singing out across the empty sea for love.

It's almost dinnertime one day when Cantrell, in the barn, hears Rainy calling. He moves out of one of the stalls where he sees her on the back porch thrashing her arms, beckoning him up. Spooked, he fairly lopes up to the house. She's in the kitchen, stooped over the table. "Listen," she says.

"Huh?"

"To the radio."

Cantrell groans but listens. Some sportscaster is talking about Tiger Woods and his return to golf after his fall from marital grace. "Who's this?"

"Tom Goldman."

"Who the hell is Tom Goldman?"

"No, that's who's talking, but it's not him. Listen, just listen."

Tiger's not at his old game yet. You can't have it all. And then Cantrell hears the wren sing. Reflexively, he looks toward the window. Rainy guffaws. "No," she rejoices, "it's on the radio. In Georgia. He's talking out on the golf course, and we're hearing the wren there."

"Jesus, Rainy, we got our own wren here. We're the only people in the state who don't have to run in and listen to him on the radio."

Rainy laughs on. It's not a ritual laugh or a social one; it's that one of a kind, completely untied. Cantrell stops to enjoy her as much as she's enjoying that wren in Georgia.

A week later when Rainy is off to Armstead for supplies, a troop of birders arrive in a van, headed by a woman in her eighties. Carol Mason claims to have identified more birds in the state than any other person. They've driven for two days. "Three hundred and eighty one," she tells Cantrell, "and it sure would be something if I could make that three-eighty-two today." She has hard green eyes that fasten like a starfish on whatever she's looking at it. Cantrell recognizes that same glint he's, heretofore, thought of only as lust, that lean squint of desire of Rainy's, for instance, one for which he has no defense whatsoever. He follows them out under the cottonwoods just to see what it's like when Carol Mason scores.

His voyeurism pays off. He sees the shudder, hears the choke, and watches that little body catatonic in rapturous absorption. What takes his breath away, though, is the pretty young woman standing alongside, her lips parted and fluttering, yet silent. When she lowers her binoculars finally, mouth completely open, she takes Cantrell in with a stunned expression, her features all slumped off guard, all composure stolen. She shrugs weakly at him and then goes back for another slamming dose. It's as if she can hardly take it. When the wren vanishes, Carol Mason leaps onto Cantrell and clasps her bony arms around him. This is an ecstasy he's never imagined before as anything but religious.

One of the men asks him with genuine awe what it's like to have a state record show up at your own home. "Let's see," Cantrell says, wanting to neither lie or disappoint, "winning something you don't need because you're the millionth customer." He winces at the blank reaction he gets. "Something like that," he tries.

That afternoon when he hears the wren singing in the orchard, he goes out on his own birding expedition with Rainy's binoculars. Although the apple trees have begun to leaf out, he finds the wren quickly and gets a good thirty seconds watching this pinpoint of other people's pleasure. He feels like he's looking at the Hope diamond, awed by its beauty but diminished by it as well, a diamond that by his measure could be glass. He's a little jealous of those who can bring so much to an experience. When he goes back in the house, Rainy is doing her wild goose Qigong. He stands in the kitchen mostly obscured by the doorframe and watches her arrested ballet with a pleasure God might envy.

The judge is a woman, and Cantrell watches her for clues, whether she dislikes Rainy because Rainy has no regard for an authority like her own, or if she likes Rainy because Rainy is Rainy. The judge takes her glasses off and cleans them. She stares at the back of the courtroom, and Cantrell doesn't know if she's even listening. She gives Rainy three months with a four-day interim to put her affairs in order.

Absurdly cheerful, Rainy uses most of those few free days to cook up and freeze meals for Cantrell. "Food's the least of it," he tells her when he drives her in to surrender herself. In the big hallway, he and Rainy hug, they kiss, and then the jail guard leads her away. Cantrell stands there in disbelief, as if he never really believed it would happen. He's not made for this sort of thing. Thank God, he's thinking when he finds himself walking back to his truck; thank God, he's got eight years on her. Ultimately, he will not be the one abandoned.

Almost three months to the day after the wren came, he disappears. Cantrell knows it when he wakes. He listens all day long, but he knows. It doesn't seem to Cantrell the bird's left, not after this much tight loyalty to a place. He guesses one of the little hawks or owls that plague the birdfeeder took him. It scares Cantrell, the immensity of this other emptiness. Rainy gets out in twenty-four days. She'll ask him, of course, the second or third question when he goes to visit. He'll tell her that he had eggs, toast, and turnips that morning, and she was right there with him, that there are still a few things he can keep from changing or leaving.

# FOUR KINDS OF FORGETTING

The day Skolly has his stroke, he's out with Connor and Marian gathering rock. The trio has gotten out of the truck to look at a boulder. "It's too big, Connor," Marian says.

"Yeah, but look at it," Connor says.

"It's too big."

"Think how it would look in your wall," Connor insists. "Just let me feel it with the bar." He goes back to the truck, retrieves the digging bar, returns, stabs it under a lip of the big rock, and pries. Like a giant tortoise awakening, the lifting boulder pulls away from the hem of sod surrounding it. "I'll be damned," Skolly says. This is the first time he's gone out with them to get rock.

"But it'll take forever," Marian says.

"Picture it at the corner," Connor says, "with a beret of Firecracker Phlox."

Skolly watches on, imagines her imagining, as she makes a humming sound, lifts her eyebrows. She's wearing a red blouse, the color of her flower. *Mimulus lewisii*—the red monkey flower—lives along fast tumbling water.

Averaging the conflict of their hand signals, Connor backs the flatbed up to the boulder. They unload the ropes and planks, then gather a small pile of melon-sized rocks. Connor uses one for a fulcrum and levers the boulder up. On her knees, Marian pushes another rock beneath. Following her lead, Skolly squats on the other side of the bar and pushes a rock under from there. Working thus, they angle one end of the boulder up, then slide two of the planks beneath and prop their other ends on the truck bed. Marian threads the ropes over and under the boulder and ties the ends to the bumper.

"This one's going to break the planks," she says.

"Naw." Connor slips the ropes through the stake pockets on either side of the truck bed, takes up the slack on one side and hands an end to Skolly. Skolly's got fifteen years on them. Marian pulls the other rope tight and waits while Connor plunges the bar in under the lowermost edge of the stone and levers forward. The rock edges up one plank. Marian takes in the slack. "One more," he says. He eases off and the rock holds. He sets the bar again and gets another couple of inches of movement up the plank. Marian cinches the rope and then watches as Connor repeats the process on Skolly's side.

Skolly keeps the rope tight, but the plank on his side is bowing badly. "She's right," he says. "I don't think it'll take the weight."

Connor inspects it. In his mid-forties, physically he is a paradox—wiry with an aura of certain strength yet feminine in the delicacy of his movement, his hands lifted slightly. He says, "Let's try another bump."

"See how Connor listens," she says. Her black bangs flutter in the breeze. Skolly watches her.

"It's either that or give up," Connor says.

"So break the plank."

Connor sets the bar and levers. The plank buckles with a sound like rifle fire. The boulder flips off, rests on an edge. "Damn," he says.

Marian, pursing her lips, shoots a victory glance at Skolly.

"Damn," Connor says again.

Marian drops the rope, hoists herself up to sit on the edge of the flatbed. Connor won't look at her lording it over him.

"Why don't you take Marge out?" Marian had asked Skolly when he called that morning. Friend Marge works at the fish hatchery. "Bring her along today."

"Quit trying to mate me. You can't drive four in a pickup anyway." Francine, his wife of twenty-nine years, has been gone now for fourteen months. Seventeen have passed since the diagnosis.

Connor tilts his head, as if catching the boulder in the right perspective will tell him what to do. "Should've put the jack under that plank. Why didn't you tell me to do that, Skolly?" Connor picks up the broken board.

They turn at the sound of an approaching truck. Connor kicks the ropes off the gravel lane. A loaded logging truck rounds the corner above, slows to pull around them, but then stops alongside, brakes hissing and squealing.

The driver leans out his window. "Trouble?"

"No," Connor says. "We were just trying to collect this rock."

The man's brows pinch. Skolly can read his perplexity. Connor is gathering the rope, his long hands and fingers trailing flourished wakes; there's the womanly tilt his head always seems to take, the way his hip tilts.

"It's for a wall," Marian says. "A kind of rock-garden wall in my yard."

The man's eyes snag on her. "That's a lotta rock." He says the word *raw-ock* with a dipthong slur of contempt. Skolly knows the look: the man is wondering what she's doing in the company of a middle-aged Peter Pan like Connor and an old gaffer. My yard—that's what the driver picked up on.

"What're you going to do?" Skolly asks her.

Connor wends around the back of the truck, strips the other

rope out of the stake pocket and begins coiling it. "Pat it on the head and drive away," she says. The rock is pocked and belted with grooves, striped and splotched with pincushion clumps of virescent moss on a surface of gouged, obdurate black.

"I can put that in for you," the truck driver says to Marian.

Connor lays the rope on the truck bed. In tandem, the three of them consider the self-loader folded over the cab and the front end of the logs. "That would be nice," she says.

The driver sets his brake, opens the door of the still idling truck and climbs to the top of the cab, where he seats himself before a panel of levers. Accompanied by a sudden squeal, the goose-necked jaws unfold and dip directly to the boulder. The forceps nudge the rock level, then mouthing it gently, lift it like an egg. When the boulder clunks down on the flatbed, the truck creaks and rolls. In moments, the driver has repackaged his steel mantis and dismounted to the ground. He joins the trio to examine the rock.

"So where do I go to see this in your yard?" he asks Marian. She gives him directions without looking at him.

The truck departs, its roar fading below in the canyon.

Skolly turns to get in the cab, but that's when the earth banks, the horizon upends. He finds himself on his back, Marian bent over him. Then it's all piecemeal, in the jouncing truck, the clunk of the boulder rocking in the bed, a wheelchair banging across a threshold at the emergency room, the white-sheeted bed in a white-sheeted room, a square of whitened sky in the window. Complicated flashbacks, intact as continental fragments, drift by in purview.

One memory plays out in the detailed but mesmeric sequence of its happening, a trip that was…how many years past? He and Connor, after mounting a ridge on Black Butte, happened onto a small swale bound on all sides by heaps of dark, broken stone.

The little basin, supplied by a seep it seemed, was awash with blue flowers—-lupine, forget-me-nots, and phacelia—a punched-out disk of sky. Butterflies stuttered the mid-summer breeze. Skolly could not imagine how these bits of weightless color kept from being blown into the next county. The current that capped the ridge carried the insects downwind, out over the flowers, where they dipped flickering, dived down and tagged the blooms. And that's how it worked. Beneath this lid of wind going away, an eddy returned just above the flowers. The butterflies' trick was to move up or down to change lanes. In the lower current, a few winked their way toward Connor and Skolly.

The two men stayed on the ridge, staircased their way upward until the blue island became a droplet edging other larger, more distant meadow expanses farther below. "It was somewhere around here," Skolly said. He zigzagged the ridge, peering over opposite edges. He could've been looking for something he'd dropped, but a flower was what he wanted, a gentian he'd seen there the year before but hadn't identified. He stopped to join Connor gazing out into the expanse, vertical volumes of emptiness heaped higher than mountains. One could almost hear cirrus ice tinkling in the jet stream. A pair of ravens materialized, two marks kiting and calling as they made their tally, checking off significant points on the horizon.

Where the ridge relented to a leveling among benchlike slabs of rock, Skolly found a clump of *Townsendia montana*, miniature asters only several inches tall with full-sized, lavender blossoms. "I'm taking one of these for Francine's rock garden," he told Connor. He dumped his pack, got down on his hands and knees, nose to the clump.

"Snack time?" Connor asked. By virtue of some orographic magic, this eyrie was windless, and the sun suddenly seemed a few million miles nearer. Connor took off his windbreaker and sat on it. Skolly lifted out one of the plants on the blade of his digging tool. He inserted the plum-sized gravel clump in a plastic sandwich bag, wrapped it, then snugged it with a rubber band, the oversize blossom wagging its head side to side. He held it up as one would a jewel and then zipped it into a front pouch of his daypack. Rifling in his pocket, Skolly took out some coins, extracted a Sacajawea dollar, and then buried it in the small hole where the plant had been.

"Thanks for the flower, is it?" Connor said. "Where'd you learn that?"

"I don't know."

They ate crackers mashed with brie, kalamata olives, dried figs, and jerked venison. Skolly uncapped a tiny flask. "To *Townsendia montana*," he says.

Connor sipped, arched his brows.

"*Eau de vie framboise*, a raspberry brandy." They passed it back and forth.

Connor studied the lower slopes of the mountain and noted, "We can see the aspen glade where the cabin is." He looked through his binoculars.

"Can you see the women?"

"No."

"Look southwest. I know one of the places they were going was a draw a mile or so below the cabin. Francine wanted to look for an *Agoseris* there."

Connor's face vanished within his blinkering hands. Mr. Mist Maiden, Skolly thought, that's his flower. Small white blossoms and the green bracket glommed to the face of a wet, black cliff. *Romanzoffia sitchensis*. Both sides, Connor is, see, like the delicate flower in front, the cliff of rock behind. Connor wiped at one eye, then resumed his search.

"You see them?"

"No."

A raven called from somewhere below. "So...you and Marian ever going to get hitched?" Skolly asked. "Or even just live together?" He sipped from the flask. It seemed a moment for a big question, now that he'd nailed Connor's flower, his totem.

"Huh?" Pulling his face away, Connor left his binoculars shelved out against the grand sky.

"It's a custom among most people of the world. After a certain preliminary stage, you know."

"Never been much for customs. Marian and I."

"Afraid of them?"

"Heck no. No more than playing Russian roulette."

"Everybody falls in love with Marian, you know."

"Yeah, but it's the kind of love you measure with hash marks."

"What's that mean?"

"They just want to collect her. Like an experience. A rafting trip, say."

"You can't disparage passion. You, of all people."

"I'm not. I'm *talking* about passion."

The ravens passed above them, their wing beats making a crisp sound, like the creasing of heavy paper. "I suppose some must think you're a waste for her."

"I probably am."

Skolly watched the ravens. They were diving, flipping side to side, showing the breadth of their backs, then disappearing when sideways they turned into slits. Venetian blinds. They pulled up, rocketing, coasting to stillness at their zenith, then plunged again.

"You think I'm wasting her time?" Connor asked.

"Some things you can't take apart, you know."

"You can take anything apart you want, so long as you've got the stomach to look at what's inside."

"Yes. Here." Skolly handed him the hip flask. "Kill it."

In the hospital, Skolly can hear Marian and Connor talking. Also a woman whose voice he doesn't recognize. She's saying: "Not that either. For a minute or so, all the old him is there, ready to go. But then he loses his train of thought. He doesn't have a train, just boxcars all loose without any hitches, and that's what's broken." Skolly opens his eyes, but when he sees it's snowing outside, flakes moving at a slant across the window, he closes them again.

In one of those boxcars, winter passes. Skolly can see daffodils nodding alongside the parking lot. A first petal has just fallen from a bouquet of tulips on the windowsill. He's being guided out the door and then down a hallway. He passes a bulletin board featuring three photos of old men under a marker-penned title "In Memoriam."

Ah yes, welcome to the Veteran's Home, Skolly thinks. Here we are. They pass an office where a man and a woman bend over a computer and point at its screen, and then the cafeteria, wide and spacious, where several of the kitchen crew are sweeping and wiping tables. A ceramic clatter of dishes issues from somewhere. In the next room with an open door, an old man plays an accordion. Perched on a stool, the miniature figure is dwarfed by the cowboy hat he wears and by his instrument. Lips working, he scrutinizes a music sheet on a stand. His short legs dangle. Down the side hall, Skolly sees a red line painted on the floor, the boundary where his bracelet sounds a buzzer and sends handlers after him.

And then they're in a large room with several television sets, a half dozen plastic-sheeted Lazy Boys, and three card tables. A man in a wheel chair sleeps, his head and arms sprawled across one table, his mouth open, lips sagging and pendant. Four others play cards at another table, a strange game, it seems, gapped with intervals of stillness, all of the men snagged by the same pause button. A baseball game without sound displays balletlike images on the screen. At the third table is Marian and, of course, Connor.

Marian is the picture of vigor. Always is. She went in the lake, but the rest of them wouldn't follow. Too cold for Skolly. For Francine, modest reserve reined in the company of these other two comparative youngsters. Skolly sits.

"How about some peanuts?" Marian asks him.

"Let's have some peanuts," Skolly says.

She leans from her chair and lines up eight peanuts alongside Skolly's foot. Moving deliberately with obvious concentration, he folds down over his lap and gathers two peanuts, then sits up and eats them. He bends again for another pair and continues until they are gone. He looks at Marian. At the lake, she had no reserve and no clothes.

If Francine did have her reserve, it was only part of an intrinsic dignity. She was no prude, discrete perhaps. Everything had a setting, that was all. *Eritrichum* was her totem. Francine Forget-me-not. *Eritrichum*, she said, not *Eritrichium*. Weber, nineteen eighty-seven, she instructed, if you want the citation. That was her native composure, hardy and high-altitude. She thrived on the wind-swept ridges. But you couldn't transplant *Eritrichum*; it refused the move. Francine didn't like the city, and she didn't care for traveling far. Certain, she was, fixed and fastidious, a place for everything and everything in its place (the university herbarium, look at the organization there), all the tidy perimeters and surfaces (just like that little blue rosette) and always on time. But she was ready for an impulse, just the same. One pantleg off up there, and then, what the hell? All of it off, under the sky. Spontaneous lust in the right places, on her naked backside in the scree with only a shirt spread beneath, herself beneath as well, the place she favored, where she could lift her pelvis and legs, angle the right fit, swallow him to the hilt, all fulcrum and full rhythm, and then afterwards shameless and giddy, still naked showing off the scalloped print of stones pressed into the long muscles of her buttocks and thighs, presenting it all to the nutcrackers winging above and any of four valleys flying out below, outrageous and elegant somehow the way she held her canted lines against the Beartooth wind, she was all levers and lashing, a sailboat, a kite.

Later, she ran laughing with him across the glacier when the storm chased them down, into the wind-slanted tent, loops of wet hair across her nose and cheeks, the two of them sitting cross-legged facing each other, watching the flares, flinching at the detonation with the forget-me-not happiness of a moment, lightning lit. And home, at mid-morning, when the kids were back in school, anywhere in the house then, so long as they could count on the dog barking if anybody showed up, whereupon the two of them each hopped around on one leg, pants all knotted up, while someone stood on the stoop thinking, their car's here.

"We have some photos," Connor says, extracting an envelope from his pocket.

Skolly sneaks a peek at the television. The Yankees and somebody. "Good."

"Your friends from Forestry sent them."

"Good."

"Who's this?" Marian hands him the top photo.

"That's Walter, his wife, Claire."

"Who else?"

"Me." He hears himself shout, lifts a hand to moderate himself.

"Where are you?"

"On top of Stenson Peak."

"It says Carrier Peak."

"Carrier Peak," Skolly barks.

He grabs for the next photo, but she draws it back. He stares at her. Is she mocking him? He could be a dog. Maybe an intractable one.

Francine knew there was a chunk of him she couldn't have, that he couldn't relegate, but she never asked, because she didn't want to hear it, no more than he wanted her to hear it. What else was he to do with that red monkeyflower coursing inside him like blood? Connor said that you can take anything apart, so long as you've got the stomach to look inside.

Connor gives him a second photo.

"*Hypericum formosum,*" Skolly says.

"Commonly known as?"

"St. Johnswort. This one is a native."

"Do you like this flower, Skolly?" Marian asks.

"Yes."

"Where do you remember seeing it?"

"It likes wet places." He cranks around to look at the television.

"Who's playing?" she asks.

"Yankees."

"Who else?"

He doesn't answer.

Connor looks unhappy, like someone who might throw up but hasn't a clue where the bathroom is. He hates it here, Skolly knows. He keeps watching the frozen card players.

"How'd you sleep last night?" Marian asks Skolly.

"Good."

"They said you went for a walk last night. Or tried to. You set off the buzzer."

"Would you like to get out of here, Skolly?" Connor asks. Marian frowns at him.

"I sure would," Skolly says.

"But you like it here, don't you, Skolly?" Marian leans at him.

He looks in her eyes, then tries to crawl back out. He imagines himself exiting one bus and getting on another. "Yes," he says. "When's lunch?"

"You just had lunch," Connor tells him.

"No, I didn't," he returns.

"How about a game of blackjack?" Marian proposes.

"Blackjack," Skolly says.

Marian extracts a deck of cards and a bottle of buttons from a cloth bag. He can see she's got two books in there, too, but she's not taking them out yet. She counts out fifteen buttons for each player and then deals, turning a nine for herself. Connor puts his hand on his cards, a king showing. "I'm fine," he says.

"Hit me," Skolly says. She adds a three to his seven. "Hit me," he says again. She deals him a four. "Hit me," he says again. She gives him an eight. "Too much," he says. He pushes his cards away, and then stretching, ganders off over his shoulder at the baseball game.

"*Bete noir*," Marian says.

"Dark beast," Skolly tells her, turning back.

"I knew you'd know," she says. She turns to Connor. "Do you remember any of those esoteric words he'd find and spring on us? Boustrophendonic, remember that one?"

Connor groans, shakes his head.

"That's where words or numbers go right to left on the first line then back left to right on the next and so forth. The root word refers to bovine, the back-and-forth way oxen plow a field. Where did you find words like that?" Marian asks.

Skolly doesn't say anything. He joins Connor in watching the old veteran asleep at the next table, the man's breathing strangled, his lips twisted like strands of rope. The only death that counts, Skolly wants to say, is the death of memory. He looks at the television, and that Yankee pitcher. Someone should turn the sound on; otherwise it will all go away, and he'll have to start over, find out who they're playing and what inning and what's happening.

"Skolly," Connor asks, rallying, "do you remember that time in Anton's cabin when it snowed on the Fourth of July?"

"Yep."

"When Marian got all those nice photos of shooting stars and blue bells and old-man-of-the-mountain, all buried in snow, poking out a little, those cards she made and sold by the bucketloads?"

"Yep."

"Remember those awful pancakes I made, when I dumped in the cocoa? You remember what happened to them?"

"Marmots wouldn't eat them." Hell yes, Skolly thinks, I can remember it as well as you can.

Connor's smile is a little goofy. But Mr. Mist-maiden has brought no treats today. Not even a square of chocolate. Francine's doing, her ghost. God, Skolly, you're getting fat, that's what she'd say if she were alive. But Francine's gone, and any minute now, Marian and Connor will be gone, too, and he'll be alone with these fresh Polaroid memories of Mimulus, unfinished, unfinishable. And then she'll leave, too, and it will be television until he gets lost. In the dark, he'll look for Francine, for Marian, for himself with them, in all the ways. Until that gets lost, too. And then it's just dark and him waiting.

"Do you ever get ideas about this?" Marian asks. She shows him his plant book. "About writing a new edition?" He tells her, yes. Yes, he thinks. But he doesn't tell her he forgets certain things, all the connections. She already knows it, Marian does. She's red and black, her black hair, her colors, herself along the water, the stream, and the inlet at that lake. *Mimulus lewisii*, where the spray beads on fuschia-colored blossoms. Wet along the snow-melt, Marian's legs and back naked going in the lake, the way her buttocks tuck that berm into her thighs, breasts flung out when she breaks back lunging, kicking the water, clear marbles and dollops fountained around her knees. The glistening black triangle below her belly, perched on the hill, softly capped, the steep mesic descent between her legs. Blossoms jerking, jittering, breezing over the water noise.

"And this," she says, "I brought your journal. I didn't know I had it all this time with your books. Do you want me to read any of it to you?"

"Read it."

She pages through. "I haven't looked in it, because...you know. I see there are dated entries." She squints, tightens into it. He can see her sudden interest. She goes to the back of the journal and pages forward, then stops. "Skolly, this is the entry for the day before your stroke."

"Read it."

"I don't know." She looks at Connor. "I see the word sex at the top. This is personal stuff."

"Read it," Skolly says.

She looks at Connor. "Go ahead," he says.

She reads in a hushed voice. "'If sex is a hundred parts, I know something about four of the clearest and how they get to gunpowder.'" She stops.

"Read it," Skolly says. Connor shrugs.

She reads on, "'First, your secret, the place itself, and for this, a magnet pull, the most animal part of my fascination, and the least discriminating. In this you are your gender, the one who owns my hankering. Whether I want it or not, I am the dog on scent. Vulgar as it sounds, it is pure, without morality, and could not be any more refined, a pure element.'" She looks up.

"Whoa," Connor says.

"There's more."

"Read it," Skolly says.

She takes a deep breath. "What's bigger is next, of course, the part that is you, the way you look and laugh, your rage, how you are when you are in charge or when you're sleepy or excited . . .'"

Skolly finds himself remembering the time when Francine lit into him after he shot a Roman Candle onto the roof of her folk's barn. And Marian in her Halloween costume, the witch who could not be wicked, all that black snuffed by dimples.

"'The standing-there-and-looking place,'" Marian reads on, "where the secrets of your nakedness are imagined, your story estimated. There's courtship when at first courtship doesn't even know it is courtship. Then the gun goes off somewhere, we both hear it, and the sprint is on. We burn down the house when it's clear to both of us what we're going to do, and that's the third part. Having it, taking my fill, this feeding heart filling the ache,'" Marian slows a little.

"'And last, not simply what you offer, not just what we are together, but what you take, your greed,'" she reads falteringly, "'hands pulling at my backside, your twisting and wrapping, gathering me, your ferocity. I can never quite get myself completely around all that, wolf answering wolf. I'm not just the question but an answer, too, something I can never quite believe.'" Marian closes the notebook on her finger, straightens, looks at neither of them, her gaze without focus. She opens it again. "And this little note," she says. "'Mimulus, I am haunted.'" Marian fixes upon him, her face slanting back, so she's peering at him over her cheeks. "*Mimulus?* Monkey flower?"

"Yes," Skolly says.

"Oh." She closes the journal. Her lips work a little. "That was your pet name for Francine?"

Skolly looks at Connor then back at her. "Yes."

"That's really sweet," she says.

They look at him like a book just closed. Suited for the shelf. Love and lunch. That's how he would have it now. They would have lunch afterward, the four of them. Bread and cheese, olives, prosciutto, a bottle of port. He will slice the bread and cheese. She will let him watch her profile.

Are you hungry? I'm famished.

Yes, yes, yes, time to go, he knows. They've got to be leaving. It was time to go before they even got here. Bye, Skolly says, good bye. That's it. He's dwelling on nothing. He doesn't even watch them going down the hall. Done, they're already gone.

Hold it. Not true. There they are, crossing the lawn under the Chinese elms. Skolly leans toward the window, because Connor has fished something from his pocket. He rubs it, polishes it on one sleeve. A coin. Marian's not noticing. She's in front. Connor stoops, pushes the coin on edge into the sod. He's standing looking down, and Marian's stopped now, turned. Connor catches up. Somebody's turned the sound on for the ball game, but Skolly can't hear the words, because he's so full of melancholy. And then like everything else, it too, leaves. Sadness doesn't stick any better than anything else.

# DIFFERENT PEOPLE'S BEES

"No Solicitors." The sign is stapled to the gatepost with an additional admonition scrawled beneath: *Or missionaries or anybody else we don't already know.* It's eight in the evening, and the serene chirrup of robins carries across the grounds from a creek beyond the fence. The bee man's place looks like the grounds of a warehouse with a home latched to the edge. A ratty caragana hedge along the gravel with a Chinese elm dead center are stand-ins for landscaping.

Caryl Denton comes to the door. He's white haired with a large belly and chest, a single curving keel that mirrors the shape of his face, large brows and nose and lips profiled like a scimitar. It's clear from his expression he's not pleased she's somebody he doesn't already know. "I'm Olivia Parker," she hurries, "and I bought Tom Lundt's hives."

A revised intentness flares across his features. "You paid the two hundred a hive he was asking?"

"Yes, I did."

"I told him he'd never get that much. I thought he was putting funny weed in his smoker."

"You're saying I've been duped?"

"You got your reasons, I spose. But making a living can't be one of them."

"I'm doing it for fun," she says. He doesn't smile. He seems in a holding pattern instead, as if he can't firm up an opinion yet. "I'm wondering if I can go out with you to learn more and watch you work?" she asks directly. Her practiced script.

"Teach my competition?"

"I can't be any threat to you."

"Showing you anything would take more time than you'd ever save me. I already got my own crew."

"I won't take up your time. I've kept three hives for a few seasons. Let me look over your shoulder for a little while, and then I'll do what you need done. For nothing."

He doesn't say anything.

"I'm good at finding queens, and that's always useful."

"You're not built for commercial work." He looks her over. "Lifting and lugging, bent over all day. I don't want to get sued for your dinged-up back."

"I'd never sue anybody," her voice lifts. "I don't think like that. I can write you up something, if you want."

"Where do you young people get the money to buy a couple hundred overpriced hives outright?"

"I used my savings. I cashed in my retirement fund. And I borrowed."

"Without any commercial experience, you got no sense to be sticking your neck out like that."

"It's none of your business how I manage money. Or my life. We both know that I'm willing to take more chances than somebody like you." She steps off the stoop. "Tom Lundt warned me about coming over here."

"Got your back up, do ya?"

She glares at him.

"Your spunk's worth something, I spose," he says. "All right, give me your phone number," he follows with an abrupt weariness. Equivocating, she regards him and then provides the number. He writes it in a little notebook drawn from his shirt pocket. "Doesn't mean I'll call," he murmurs, his voice strangled a little in the folds of his down-turned neck.

"Does it mean you won't?"

"What?" He looks up, snaps his ballpoint.

She walks away.

Olivia left her adjunct professor position with the university in Armstead and moved to Fletcher when she found the small, sideline honey business for sale. She had other work as a scientific editor, free-lancing part time at home, also as a disease inspector for bees, a job she'd wangled by way of a colleague in the state Ag department. Piecemeal as her new livelihood was and would be, she had no regrets leaving academia. It wasn't the regime of worthy challenges she'd expected, a form of deprivation instead, compartmental and hermetic. People burrowed away from each other, specialized themselves out of view. If money wasn't the measure of surrogate success, then it was vitae stuffed with anything in reach—seven co-authors, for instance, on a one-page journal article with more words in the title than in the text. The parleying for advantage never involved more than what any two dogs did when they met. She was having no fun and going nowhere of any consequence, not beneath the wide sweep of sky.

On the outskirts of campus, she'd maintained three hives of bees for basic study by the biology classes and for experimental work by students in Animal Behavior. She knew how to diagnose diseases, how to counter swarming, and in theory, how to manage them for maximum honey production. She fell in love with the bees because their sociality and powers of discrimination were just as reliable as they were complicated. In the Animal Behavior labs, the demonstrations with bees always worked; several showed how their dances described the location of food and others revealed what colors, designs, and fragrances the insects could distinguish among. Similar examinations of other creatures, mostly vertebrates—considered far more advanced than insects—usually ended up as post mortem analyses of failure.

She loved the colonies themselves: the smells of honey and flowers mingled with that of pine in the leaking pitch of the woodware; the oblivious dedication of the creatures themselves, the way they banged into her leaving and returning to the hive, or their coded dances on the side of the comb proceeding on in the sunlight as she examined them; or the queen poking around looking for an empty cell, swapping ends, lowering her egg-swollen abdomen and making her deposit; that deposit itself wondrously controlled where she dotted the smaller worker cells with fertilized eggs or withheld the sperm bagged up within her to set out unfertilized eggs in the larger cells for drone larvae, and above all, the colony's resolute vitality and dependability. After Olivia saw to it that they were queen-right and free of disease, supplied with stores during periods of stress, and provided with space before they were crowded, she had only to stand back and watch them load in honey for her to take, a single colony sometimes burgeoning with a surplus equal to her own weight, a hundred twenty-five pounds gathered by a single family of insects.

In Fletcher, she bought two hundred hives from a beekeeper who was retiring from retiring. A decade earlier Tom Lundt downscaled from a thousand, selling eight hundred colonies to Caryl Denton, his rival in the valley. Olivia had only met Lundt once in the fall to survey the seven remaining yards and their hives; by the time she took over in the spring he'd moved to Arizona. He instructed her to write or call with any questions, and without any context whatsoever, supplied the caveat that Caryl Denton was an impossible human being, and that she'd want to keep her distance from him.

In March, she began her rounds in an old Forest Service Ford pickup, a flatbed truck that came with the deal (along with a 1956 International one-and-a-half-ton with a hydraulic tailgate lift). Within hours of her first day's work, she realized how poorly she'd extrapolated from three hives to two hundred. A half hour on each hive times two hundred came out at two and a half weeks work, which left little time for editing, inspecting, or anything else before she had to start the next round through the hives again. Momentarily stupefied, she stood among the colonies with smoke drifting into her face and a few chilled bees bumbling across the front of her veil. How did anyone manage a thousand colonies?

Her late calculation made it clearer why Lundt wouldn't sell on terms. He didn't want to foreclose later on mismanaged ruins. The only projection she'd made was in figuring how much honey she could expect from two hundred hives, what she'd be taking to market. She looked around at the moribund yard under a rain-smelling sky and, in another dismal calculation, figured that if she toughed it out and stayed till this yard was done, she'd be closing the gate at about three in the morning.

"Don't stand in front of the hive. Don't set your hive tool down," Denton inveighs. He looks like a bear in his bee suit, a polar bear wearing a veil. "You spend all day looking for it. A bee-keeper eats his lunch with his hive tool in his hand."

"Her hand?"

"You already calling yourself a beekeeper?"

"Seems to me anybody with the bee troubles I've got gets to call herself a beekeeper."

"Only if you can fix them instead of making them worse," he says. "Beekeeper not bee killer." She can't read his face through two veils. "So how come you don't have a boyfriend to help?" he asks at length. "You the wrong kind of woman?"

"What's the wrong kind of woman?" Open-mouthed, she lowers the tipped-up hive body and waits.

"You know what I'm talking about. A good-looker like you's gonna' have the boys dogging after her." Denton, kneeling now, goes on inspecting a frame of comb.

"Are you asking if I'm a...a lesbian? Or a man-hater?" She makes no pretense of working the hive, not when she's this distracted. "Why don't you come out and say it?"

"Don't get your dander up. Whatever's different than regular, that's all I'm asking."

"I'm not what you're thinking. But I'm not interested in men who think I've been put on this planet to have their dinner ready."

"That makes you one of them feminists, I take it?"

"You drink a glass of water, that makes you the water boy?"

This time he looks up. He snorts, then goes back to the bee-sweatered frame he's examining, the silence submerging into the soft roar of bee sound.

At the next hive, Olivia inspects the weathering on the outside of the boxes. "Some of these hive bodies need painting," she says.

"I raise bees and honey, not woodware."

"That's a bad attitude. Tom Lundt was good on maintenance. You have to give him that."

"Tom Lundt spent his whole life looking over his shoulder. When Lundt was pulling honey, he arranged his loaded truck so his best-looking supers were on the outside."

"You'd believe anything bad about Tom Lundt. How would you know that about him?"

"One of the guys who worked for him told me."

She tries to imagine someone loading their truck for appearance. Then, finding the hive matriarch, she starts. "Wo, this queen's maimed. She's only got one leg on her right side."

"What kind of brood she got?"

"Beautiful brood."

"Leave her be. I don't care if she's wearing rings through her lips so long as she's got good brood."

Olivia watches the queen drag herself in short arcs across the comb. Without context whatsoever, Denton asks, "What about that Mexican 'cross the valley?"

"Huh?"

"I've seen him around. You talked to him when he came to my place."

"So?"

"He worked bees and wants a hive. That's what you said."

"So?"

"Can't imagine he wasn't looking you over. You just dust them off? Every one that comes along?"

"I'm not answering questions like that."

Lauro, a slender man with glossy neck-length hair, had driven into Denton's turnaround in a clunker pickup. She was there alone at the time, waiting for Denton, who'd run out to Clay Creek to retrieve a half dozen nucleus hives. They introduced themselves. "La-ooo-row," he said. "Larry, if that's easier. I live on Merton Creek." He pointed off over his back. He had a long scar that diagonaled one cheek. There was something intense about him, a sprinter waiting for the gun.

"Yes," she said, "I've seen you in your garden there."

He canted his head.

"I get eggs and milk from Saunders, so I drive by your place every week."

"Ah." He nodded, clapped his hands lightly. "Where does the bee man here get his supplies?"

"You keep bees?"

"I want to start a hive."

"It's a little late this year."

"It's always a little late. I worked for a bee outfit in Texas." He folded his arms and looked around. "So's, he around?"

"No, but he's due back. You'll have to register with the state, as a hobbyist. They'll inspect you once a year."

He studied her as if she'd invited the indulgence. "You part of the family here?" he asked. "Or a worker?"

"No." She looked him up and down, reflected his liberties back upon him. But his bearing remained unhindered by her scrutiny, his lanky, easy way of standing unaffected. "I help him once in a while." She turned away and searched up the lane for Denton.

"Just help him? How's he rate?"

"For the experience," she said. "I have my own small bee business."

"Really? How many hives?"

"Two hundred."

"So you can recommend a supply house?"

"We get our stuff out of Armstead. Mosley's. I've got the address." She went to the truck, returned with an old envelope, and wrote the address on the back. "I can give you the address for registering your hives, too."

A momentary languor seemed to overtake him. "I don't think the state's going to worry about one or two hives," he said.

"Oh yeah, they will. If you don't register, you'll get reported." She scribbled on, then gave it to him.

He squinted, advanced his face a little. "Are you trying to tell me something?"

"I'm the deputy inspector for this county."

He tipped his ah-ha face at the sky. "And what's this cost?"

"Twenty dollars for up to ten hives."

"So how about I write you check for ten, and we forget there's any hives up Merton Creek?"

"That wouldn't be right, would it?"

He smiled for the first time and examined her again. Straightening finally, he said, "Look, I'm going. This address...these addresses are all I need."

"Maybe you can start a hive this late in Texas, but it won't winter here."

When he eyed her again, she could tell he didn't have his mind on bees.

In the yard with Denton, she hurries to finish the hive she's working on, thinking to move on to the next row and beyond earshot.

"What about inspecting?" Denton asks her.

"What about it?"

"How many friendly offers you get when you're out writing up other people's hives?"

"None of your business, Denton. Leave me alone. I got a mess here. The brood here is nothing but drone." She's looking at a frame of bullet-shaped cells.

"Check the eggs. See if laying workers are gobbing up more than one to a cell. If it's a regular pattern, find the queen, and kill her. There's still a nuc left."

"I know what to do."

"That's true." He pauses. "You know I could pay you something till the next round starts."

"I couldn't deal with you as a boss, Denton."

"What kind of debts you looking at?"

"Also none of your business. Dad."

"Don't Dad me. If I were ten years younger."

"Ten?"

"Twenty."

"Twenty?"

"You got a mean streak."

"What would your wife think about you talking like this?"

"Marlene has a crush on every country singer over forty," Denton says. "She'd run off with the first one who'd have her."

"She's told you that?"

"Don't miss a chance."

"She as full of it as you?" she asks.

"I'm not full of it. I wouldn't take on anybody else dumb enough to buy Lundt's dregs. Not less I liked looking at 'em bent over a hive."

"Oh boy."

"It's a crime against God to put what you got out to pasture."

"Cut it out, Denton," she drops a lid, flings it a little, "if I had a dick and balls would you leave me alone?"

He stops and gazes at her.

"What?"

"Did you mash that queen like I told you?"


Coming in the door, she hears her answering machine, her own voice clowning first, singing, "Nobody here. Nobody home. Noooobody. Leave a message."

"Lauro here," he says. "I'd like to invite you to dinner." He hesitates. "Any evening. And if you won't do dinner, then lunch or whatever works." He pauses. "I'm hanging sheet-rock on that site across from Callahan's. I see your truck go by." He waits, as if he forgot what he was going to say next. Then he hangs up.

Lauro moved up Merton Creek not long after Olivia came to Fletcher. He'd been there long enough for her to notice his imprimatur on the place, on the grounds specifically. The small house, old to begin with, aged on with white paint peeling to gray, the asphalt shingles thickening with shims of moss, its profile rounding, ovaling, like the stump of a long-gone tree, while the yard and garden transformed daily. A solar dryer and racks appeared along with a small greenhouse built off the south side of the woodshed, also several cold frames made from old window sashes. In the garden during May, cloches ribbed with arches of plastic pipe mantled recently tilled rows then vanished in July to reveal surprisingly robust vines of cucumber, watermelon, and canteloupe. The raspberries, pruned of all the old canes, arced out over railings made of trussed-together lodgepole. A knoll of strawberries, a tangled mass one week, turned into a weeded checkerboard whitened with blossoms the next. Sugar-snap peas adorned two fences seven or eight-feet tall, while fava beans got lashed to a waist-high fence. In later summer, the hills of pumpkins and winter squash plants disappeared beneath one nearly level awning of large palmate leaves.

When she drives in and walks up the path to the front door, she's struck by the womanly ambience of the place: flower boxes loaded with dwarf yellow marigolds and sky-blue lobelia, planters with begonias and geraniums in wild shades of lipstick, a hummingbird feeder thrumming with flourished arrivals and departures, evanescent calligraphy. A heron carved from driftwood searches for fish among yellow and purple pansies.

Gardening will get its due in her life again, once she gets a little piece of time on each end of the day. Dinking-in-the-garden-time. She knocks on the screen door, each blow echoing as the frame strikes the doorway. She loathes her fraudulence. He's not home, and she knows it, for she's waited until his truck was gone. Why the charade? She finds the hive behind the woodshed. He's set it upon two cinder blocks, two hive bodies freshly painted light blue, a make-shift lid covered with an aluminum press-plate, a brick atop that. Bees are streaming in and out steadily, a surprising abundance for a hive in the June of its first season. What is it about this guy, his Midas touch for living things? How does anybody get a three-pound package of bees to fill two hive bodies so fast?

When she pops the inner cover she doesn't find the blonde, fresh pine she expects but rather dark wood with chocolate-brown comb, all stained with propolis. A mantle of orange dandelion-stained bees flows in various directions. She has to puff more smoke because the hive, loaded with bees, four or five pounds possibly, bristles with morale. She draws out a frame of brood. The cappings or papery cover over the pupating larvae is a shade lighter than the comb, a texture like bark parchment. The corners of the frames' top bars are square cut. Home-made woodware, seasons old. She makes a quick perusal for foulbrood, closes the hive, and fills out her inspection book, rips loose the duplicate, and tucks it into the handle of the screen door. Brooding, she drifts over to the vegetable garden to see what miracles he's enlisted there.

*

Denton has no greeting. He was about to leave a message when she picked up the phone. "Tell me," he blurts, "who would steal brood frames from a hive but leave the rest?"

"What?"

"And then, get this, stick new frames with foundation in place of where he took them."

"He? Do you know who it is?"

"Jesus Christ, you didn't do it, did you?"

"No, but I'm not the only woman in the world."

"What the hell. How many women you inspected?"

"Not many."

"How many?"

"Not any yet, I guess."

"Like I said, why would he do that? Why wouldn't he just steal what he wanted? Take the goddamn hive?"

"Maybe they didn't feel like stealing outright. Maybe they'd built their equipment and then decided afterwards to make the trade. Maybe they did it in the way that would cost you the least. Did they take all the frames from the same hive?"

"No, two from each of four hives. Stealing is stealing, for Christ's sake."

"Are the replacement frames built well? What kind of foundation?"

"Wired, just like mine, none of that plastic shit. But he walked off with eight damn good frames of brood. How would you like it? You come home, your TV dinner is gone, and somebody's left you a fish. With the guts still in and the scales still on."

"It would bother me."

"Damn rights. Keep an eye out for my frames, will you? When you're inspecting? It's easy to tell they're mine because I sawed them out. They're not factory mades, but you know that. The ones he stuck in got those skinny little end bars."

"Listen, Denton, I wouldn't be surprised if you go back in a month and find they've switched them back again and the new stuff is gone."

His breathing is loud and rapt. "Oh, and his frames will have the comb drawn and filled with eggs and larvae ready to take to all those nurse bees and hatched brood he got away with on the first switch." He makes a low, descending whistle. "If he had it timed right, I'da never've known. If he'd squeezed it just right, I mean, between rounds."

"Sure. They're probably thinking what you don't know won't hurt you."

"I could booby trap one of them hives if he's coming back. Hot wire it to a transmission line, and fry that sucker straight up and down."

"I'll bet they never bother you after this, Denton."

"How the hell would you know?"

"I'm only trying to think like a petty bee thief."

He doesn't answer. She can hear the bellows of his respiration.

"Oh boy," she says after he hangs up.

Lauro calls not long after Denton has. She listens to him on the recorder. "So you came to look me over, Olivia Parker. Tell me, you ever seen chile plants like that before, anchas, serranos, habaneros? You saw them didn't you? Around the corner from the delphiniums?" He waits, as if listening. "You should let me cook you a relleno, because you've never had a relleno like mine. They'll be ready in August." He pauses. "So, my hive…now you know one of my little secrets. I wonder if Mr. Denton knows. I've seen him in his truck and at the Post Office, but I haven't met the man yet. You know, don't you, how little I've taken from him, and how much he's given me? A year with bees. You can't buy a year with bees." Again, he hesitates. "And you, when will you give in and enjoy food like you've never had it?" He waits as if she'll answer, the long stillness haunted until, at length, he hangs up.

She shivers, pushes away her plate and the remnants of cold spaghetti, then charges her teacup with another three fingers of wine. Sorting through the spill of mail on the table, she finds a pencil and extracts a junk-mail envelope. On the blank back, she composes her list. Once, all her lists on the backs of envelopes could've been entitled "To Do," but lately they've evolved to something like "What Matters and What Doesn't." By the time her cup's empty, she's got a tally to brood over. Not a good sign. It's more like a list of admissions.

In late afternoon, Lauro's truck approaches. She's working in the Donahue yard alongside Tannery Road. The frame of his pickup is bent so that it looks like a bird heading in a crosswind, pointed northwest but driving north. She turns her back to the road. She can hear the truck slow, the munching of gravel growing louder and more distinct, and then the silence until the creak of his door. "Hello, beekeeper," he calls.

She turns. "Hello. What are you doing?"

He's hunched over on the other side of the truck. When he straightens, he's zipping his bee suit, brand new and white as paper. "I'm going to help you." He grabs his veil and gloves, his hive tool and approaches the fence.

"I don't need any help. I don't want any help."

"I don't believe you." He stoops to slip between the strands of barb wire, and then zipping his veil, makes his way around the gate into her yard. "Tell me the layout, what you're doing, and I'll help you get done."

"I don't want you to help me get done."

"What are these hives with the sticks on top?"

"Go away."

"You're wasting good time. Are those the hives in trouble?"

"They're the weakest. They need help."

"And where are you getting help?"

"From the strong hives, of course. I don't have them marked but you can tell them by all the old dandelion stains at the entrances. But I'm telling you I don't—"

"You've done the first row?"

She won't answer.

"I'll start at the back then."

They watch each other, stalemated for a moment. "What are you doing there?" He looks at the hive she's taken down with frames propped everywhere.

"It's a strong hive. I'm looking for the queen, so I can steal brood."

"That's a waste of time."

"I don't want to lose any queens here. I have enough problems as it is."

"Pull frames of capped brood, check them over good, and steal them. She won't be on those frames. She's on the egg frames. If by some fluke she is, she's easy to spot."

"That's sloppy."

"Not when you look at the odds. So what if you lose a queen in fifty hives? You save twenty hours work for the price of a queen, which is what? Ten pounds of honey. How sloppy is that?"

"Ten pounds? You mean if you buy them."

"Sure, but you don't have to buy them. You can make a lot of queens in twenty hours' work."

She stands there, rooted. She can see his logic, but she doesn't like the assembly-line mechanics.

"Do it this way, and you'll never look back." He's already got a hive pulled apart, a frame of capped brood lifted high, his back to the sun.

"I'd rather put in the twenty hours than have you horning in here, lording it over me."

"Do you have a weak hive open and ready, or should I just do my own?"

"Do your own."

"Have you counted the strong ones yet?"

"No, why?"

"So you know how much you can steal to beef up the others. You don't want to go back twice."

"Why don't you get the hell out of here?"

"I'm not saying another thing. I'll stick with these three back rows and stay out of your hair."

She doesn't answer. She's not sure whether to go on looking for the queen in the hive she's working, or to cave in to his argument. In this no-woman's land, she's not reliable.

But Lauro is true to his word. For an hour, he works in silence. When the occasional neighbor drives by and honks, they both straighten and wave and then return to work. Now and then she glances at his progress. He's several hives ahead of her. If prototypic male carelessness operates, who knows how many queenless hives she'll find in the back rows of this yard on her next round? What's he going to want when he's done? Typical trick this, painting her into a corner of indebtedness. But he'll find out. Zilch, that's what she's got for him. "Did you have your own bees in Texas?" she hears herself asking.

"No. I worked for a couple of queen breeders."

"Um."

"Bees saved my life. I was in a bad place."

"What do you mean?"

"They pulled me out of a mess, a bad life."

"What kind of mess?"

"Just a mess."

They're at opposite ends of the middle row, everybody else's dinner time and a half hour or so to go, when Denton drives by. He stops, backs up, and gets out.

"Well, well," he says with lavished pomposity. "How about this?"

"He just barged his way in here, Denton. I didn't have a thing to do with it. So don't be smug."

Lauro is silent until Denton stretches over the wire to see what he's doing. "I'm Lauro Olivarez. I live up Merton Creek."

"I know who you are," Denton says. "You came by my place once. You a Mexican?"

"No, you a German?"

"You're not a Mexican?"

"I'm an American."

"Don't get your water hot. I was on your side. But she's chary of men."

Looking perplexed, Lauro folds at the waist, attends to his

ighten and wave and then return to work. Now and then...
...ces at his progress. He's several hives ahead of her. If pro...
...ic male carelessness operates, who knows how many queenle...
...es she'll find in the back rows of this yard on her next round?
...at's he going to want when he's done? Typical trick this, paint-
... her into a corner of indebtedness. But he'll find out. Zilch,
...t's what she's got for him. "Did you have your own bees in
...xas?" she hears herself asking.

"No. I worked for a couple of queen breeders."

"Um."

"Bees saved my life. I was in a bad place."

"What do you mean?"

"They pulled me out of a mess, a bad life."

"What kind of mess?"

"Just a mess."

They're at opposite ends of the middle row, everybody else's
...nner time and a half hour or so to go, when Denton drives by. He
...ps, backs up, and gets out.

"Well, well," he says with lavished pomposity. "How about
...is?"

"He just barged his way in here, Denton. I didn't have a thing
... do with it. So don't be smug."

Lauro is silent until Denton stretches over the wire to see
...hat he's doing. "I'm Lauro Olivarez. I live up Merton Creek."

"I know who you are," Denton says. "You came by my place
...nce. You a Mexican?"

"No, you a German?"

"You're not a Mexican?"

"I'm an American."

"Don't get your water hot. I was on your side. But she's chary
...f men."

Looking perplexed, Lauro folds at the waist, attends to his

"I'm only trying to think like a petty bee thief."

He doesn't answer. She can hear the bellows of his respiration.

"Oh boy," she says after he hangs up.

Lauro calls not long after Denton has. She listens to him on
the recorder. "So you came to look me over, Olivia Parker. Tell me,
you ever seen chile plants like that before, anchas, serranos, habaneros? You saw them didn't you? Around the corner from the delphiniums?" He waits, as if listening. "You should let me cook you
a relleno, because you've never had a relleno like mine. They'll be
ready in August." He pauses. "So, my hive...now you know one of
my little secrets. I wonder if Mr. Denton knows. I've seen him in
his truck and at the Post Office, but I haven't met the man yet. You
know, don't you, how little I've taken from him, and how much
he's given me? A year with bees. You can't buy a year with bees."
Again, he hesitates. "And you, when will you give in and enjoy
food like you've never had it?" He waits as if she'll answer, the long
stillness haunted until, at length, he hangs up.

She shivers, pushes away her plate and the remnants of cold
spaghetti, then charges her teacup with another three fingers of
wine. Sorting through the spill of mail on the table, she finds a
pencil and extracts a junk-mail envelope. On the blank back, she
composes her list. Once, all her lists on the backs of envelopes
could've been entitled "To Do," but lately they've evolved to
something like "What Matters and What Doesn't." By the time
her cup's empty, she's got a tally to brood over. Not a good sign. It's
more like a list of admissions.

In late afternoon, Lauro's truck approaches. She's working
in the Donahue yard alongside Tannery Road. The frame of his
pickup is bent so that it looks like a bird heading in a crosswind,
pointed northwest but driving north. She turns her back to the
road. She can hear the truck slow, the munching of gravel growing

louder and more distinct, and then the silence until the creak of his door. "Hello, beekeeper," he calls.

She turns. "Hello. What are you doing?"

He's hunched over on the other side of the truck. When he straightens, he's zipping his bee suit, brand new and white as paper. "I'm going to help you." He grabs his veil and gloves, his hive tool and approaches the fence.

"I don't need any help. I don't want any help."

"I don't believe you." He stoops to slip between the strands of barb wire, and then zipping his veil, makes his way around the gate into her yard. "Tell me the layout, what you're doing, and I'll help you get done."

"I don't want you to help me get done."

"What are these hives with the sticks on top?"

"Go away."

"You're wasting good time. Are those the hives in trouble?"

"They're the weakest. They need help."

"And where are you getting help?"

"From the strong hives, of course. I don't have them marked but you can tell them by all the old dandelion stains at the entrances. But I'm telling you I don't—"

"You've done the first row?"

She won't answer.

"I'll start at the back then."

They watch each other, stalemated for a moment. "What are you doing there?" He looks at the hive she's taken down with frames propped everywhere.

"It's a strong hive. I'm looking for the queen, so I can steal brood."

"That's a waste of time."

"I don't want to lose any queens here. I have enough problems as it is."

"Pull frames of capped brood, check them ove[r] them. She won't be on those frames. She's on the some fluke she is, she's easy to spot."

"That's sloppy."

"Not when you look at the odds. So what if y[ou] in fifty hives? You save twenty hours work for the p[...] which is what? Ten pounds of honey. How sloppy [...]

"Ten pounds? You mean if you buy them."

"Sure, but you don't have to buy them. You ca[n] queens in twenty hours' work."

She stands there, rooted. She can see his logic, [...] like the assembly-line mechanics.

"Do it this way, and you'll never look back." H[e] a hive pulled apart, a frame of capped brood lifted [...] to the sun.

"I'd rather put in the twenty hours than have y[ou] here, lording it over me."

"Do you have a weak hive open and ready, or sh[...] my own?"

"Do your own."

"Have you counted the strong ones yet?"

"No, why?"

"So you know how much you can steal to beef u[p] You don't want to go back twice."

"Why don't you get the hell out of here?"

"I'm not saying another thing. I'll stick with these rows and stay out of your hair."

She doesn't answer. She's not sure whether to go [...] for the queen in the hive she's working, or to cave in t[...] ment. In this no-woman's land, she's not reliable.

But Lauro is true to his word. For an hour, he works When the occasional neighbor drives by and honks, [...]

hive again.

Olivia feigns a concentration of her own.

"You come across my frames yet?" Denton asks, his tone idle.

"No," she says.

He looks at Lauro, but Lauro works on, oblivious apparently.

When Denton leaves, Lauro says, "How come you never told him?"

"I don't know. I still might."

Shortly, they finish. He helps her clean up, replace the rocks on the lids, close the gate, and tie down the remainder of her gear on the flatbed. "Thank you," she says. "That's all you're getting."

"Look." He raises a finger. "I got a good dinner almost ready. Heat up a few things. So come over and eat. Just eat and go home, that's all." He looks at his watch. "You can be home by eight."

"No."

"You have something else going tonight?"

"That's none of your business."

"I don't think Denton's right about you and men."

"Look, goddamn it, I'm not in the market for a relationship." She says this last word the way one might say sewage or morgue. "I've been married before. I'm not the marrying type."

"All right, but we're just talking dinner here."

"I'm not."

He goes to her truck, climbs in and starts it. Rooted, dumb-founded, she breaks too late, runs to the door, but he pulls ahead and then slows. "Goddamn it Lauro, you—"

"We'll trade trucks at my house," he calls back. "I'll give you your keys after dinner."

"You're stealing my truck," she yells. "I'll report you."

"Trading, not stealing." He slows. She walks to catch up. Twisting his head back, he says, "Pull the choke out halfway, pump the pedal twice. If it doesn't start right off, floorboard it, and grind till it catches." Then he pulls himself back in and speeds away.

She stops, waits for him to stop or turn around, to end the ridiculous prank, but he proceeds on out to the county road and then up the hill and over. She can hear the diminuendo of his unrelenting departure. She closes her mouth, labors to unbug her eyes. She'd squeeze her temples with both hands if she didn't have on her veil and gloves. Hastily, she searches about until she finds a baseball-sized rock. Snatching it up, she approaches his truck, sharpens the image of an obliterated windshield, her pitching arm swinging like a pendulum. Then she winds up and does nothing.

He's standing on the porch with her keys. "It's ready," he says, "if you give me seven more minutes."

"Give me my keys." She stretches her arm out.

"Make it take-home then. I won't give you the keys, unless you take it with you."

"I want to go right now."

"It's ready right now, if you heat it at home."

When she doesn't say anything, he dashes into the house. She can hear the sound of popping lids, the crackle of paper, sklinking foil. In moments he's back, pressing a big brown, grocery bag into both arms and the keys into her right palm. He steps back, hands lifted.

She turns away.

"Let me look at some of that old extracting equipment before you sell it. All right?"

She turns. "What? How'd you know that?"

"I wasn't snooping. Your list, it was just lying there on the seat, in your truck. I couldn't pull my eyes off. Not after number one."

"Goddamn it. You had no right to do that."

"There's good food in that sack. Either you'll like it and want to see me again. That's what I figure. Or you won't, and I'll give up."

"Is that a promise?"

"Yes."

Driving down Merton Creek Road, back in her own truck, she seeks to locate herself. She's going home to a quiet, uncluttered evening, and although the dinner is unwanted, she will make use of it—now that all strings have been cut and swept away. Besides that, the Donahue yard is done for another thirty-five days. For the moment, she's oddly free. Call it a respite.

In the kitchen she removes the yogurt and cottage-cheese containers of red and green salsa and then an orange and green concoction with the scent of garlic, ginger, and cilantro. Let's see, she's thinking, take off my bee suit first, wash up, and turn on the radio. Yes, settle in, and then I'll deal with this. But she's back in the sack again, poking around. She extracts and unrolls a cylinder of tortillas, both flour and corn, separated with squares of paper. Like a fortune from a cookie, a message slips out. 'Warm these last, cover with a towel.' She opens the silverware drawer, selects a teaspoon and opening the yogurt container again, the one redolent of herbs and spice, she dips out a half spoonful and, tasting, glances back into the bag again. There are foil-covered paper plates, something wrapped in wax paper, a Kerr jar with what looks like a grape-colored drink, most or all of them tagged with instructional messages in remarkably neat printing.

He knew she wouldn't stay. From the onset. She unfolds the foil from one of the paper plates. Then she stops. Involuntarily, Olivia Parker, sweaty and unwashed, attends to the flavors shimmering in her mouth.

# HOWARD'S END

Howard Seminski, standing one foot on the wood stove and the other on a stool, holds a can of furnace cement in one hand, squints up under the blower, and pokes at the rusted seams of stovepipe with a butter knife. When he gets a dusting in the face, he curses, blinks at the grit, and waits for it to water out. But it doesn't water out of one eye, stabs and burns instead. He goes to the bathroom, pries his clenching, squirming lids apart, and labors to slow the sympathetic blinking in the good eye. At last, prevailing over both, he subdues the red, running orb into a sort of cataleptic stillness and locates the fleck. When he tries to tease it out with a folded corner of toilet paper, the fragment seems fastened, stuck like a dagger. Thwarted, Howard stares at the mirror, doubly annoyed with the idiot annoyance staring back at him. He goes back to the stove in the front room where he tries to conjure a replay. The crooked stovepipe with the stack fan looks like a black snake that's just eaten a square egg. Returning to the bathroom, scowling terrifically, he wedges his eye open again.

Carol Remmick is the nurse at the clinic desk. "I was patching a stack robber," he tells her and waits.

"I know what a stack robber is, Howard," she says.

"Well, I managed to stick a piece of it in my eye."

She wants to see. Obediently, he lowers himself, splaying his knees. He imagines himself as a figure in a fountain, about to spew an arc of water. She comes around the counter, stands on her tip-toes, and cradling his face, peers intently into the crucible of his head. The sensation is loaded with ancient familiarity, something of when he was a boy, of his grandmother's hands maybe, and ideas of special comic-book powers, X-ray vision, pieces of memory hitherto lost. Then he's looking at Nurse Remmick's ear, her neck, her black and silver stranded hair, disbelieving their nearness. He and Carol went to school together at Fletcher High some forty years ago. "I see it," she says. "Can I try for it with my tongue?"

"What?"

"Lick it out."

"Jesus, Carol, is that what a nurse does?"

"Hold still."

He feels the soft, exploratory nub of her tongue, something he imagines nimble and exotic as the pliable, nailless finger of a marmoset.

"It's stuck," she says.

"No duh."

She jerks back, glowers.

"You think I'd come here, drive all the way to town, if I could get it out myself?" He's looking at her teeth, at their uniform array, gateway to words, commands and refusals, to a tongue that would presume to enter any eye. She lets go of his head and turns away, telling him Dr. Clement will have to extract it, that she'll get it arranged in the next little while. "Sit down," she says.

When he and Carol Remmick were in high school, Howard slid his car into hers. He apologized. She apologized. They stood there on rutted ice looking at her broken headlight and his dented fender while they waited for policeman Larry Anders to come and write it up. Reflecting back years later, Howard viewed this prolonged turmoil of mute immobility in the flying snow as his first conscription, scene one maybe, in the theater of the absurd.

Dr. Clement, Melvin Clement, is an astonishingly short man, brisk, with a W-shaped brow that suggests much is being considered within, while his mouth, puckered like a kiss, belies amusement. "A tack in your eye?" he says. They're in a room not much bigger than a closet. Howard sits on a stool. Ordinarily, these professional youngsters offer little of interest, but the doctor's diminutiveness and lingering sport, if that's what it is, make for idle study. Howard has to wonder if she told him something. Dr. Melvin applies several drops of anesthetic in Howard's eye, then rolls up a stand adorned with a mask, several lenses, and an assortment of attachments resembling tiny cranes. He tinkers with the machine. Nurse Remmick standing alongside, towering, has an air less of attending than of presiding. Howard, as directed, presses his face into the mask and fixes on a point of light. "Should've let it take care of itself." He can feel the blurry effect of the anesthetic.

"Not unless you wanted an infection. You've already got a rust stain."

"This happens to other people?"

"To mechanics. All the time…when they're under cars." He scoots his butt around like a pianist aligning himself with the keyboard. "How long you lived in Fletcher, Howard?"

"I live out on the front, under Whale Reef."

"All his life," Nurse Remmick supplies. Melvin glances at her. "We went to school together."

"Remember the time I wrecked your car?" Howard asks.

"Don't move," Melvin says, facing again, leaning in. "And don't talk either."

"You didn't wreck my car. I wrecked yours," she says.

"You, too," Melvin says.

"I will, but it's true. I ran into him. My headlight was broken."

Angling toward Howard, Melvin's motion is arrested.

"All right," she says.

"Only because I was going faster when we hit our brakes," Howard says.

The doctor sits back. "He was about to ask me out," she tells him. "Took him all fall and most of the winter to get around to it. Because I was a year older. Then that wreck scared him off. For good."

Howard has to close his mouth. He can't refute her.

"Is that true, Howard?" Melvin asks.

"Can't remember that far back. That would've been in the Cambrian."

"Yes, you can," she says with a kind of hushed vehemence.

The fervor of her certainty assumes a secret sharing, or so it seems. He has an inkling of some other life—another outcome—in a separate dimension or plane, and in this stranded moment, it's as if he just heard the snick of intersecting planes, glimpsed an alternate past sliding by.

"Howard?" the doctor says.

"What?"

"Is that true?"

Howard shrugs his brow.

The doctor leans in again. Shadows merge across the beam of light. At length, Howard registers a nudge, something small but complete. "There," Melvin says. "I got it."

Howard's standing, blinking, experimenting with his anesthetized eye, trying to see the fleck on Melvin's finger, when Nurse Remmick asks Howard if he's ever had a colonoscopy.

"What kind of question is that?" Howard snips.

Melvin seems as puzzled as Howard is irritated. He has to be a good two feet shorter, Howard guesses. Than everybody.

"Howard's father died of colon cancer when we were in our

twenties," Nurse Remmick tattles.

"That's my confidential history you're bandying around," Howard says.

"You should have that test, Howard, if you haven't." The doctor sets his jaw. Moses now, pocket-sized.

"I don't want to pay for it. I don't want to be knocked out." And he sure as hell didn't want anybody mucking around where the sun never shines.

"Howard, you're high risk," she says.

In the wondrous intricacies of an instant, he imagines her presence as a daily familiarity. "I'm ten years older than my Dad when he died, Ms. Remmick. I made it through that gate."

"Listen, Howard," the doctor says, warm, earnest, winningly offhanded, one old friend to another, "take home a card for a stool sample and mail it in. If there's no blood, we'll settle for a sigmoid-oscopy, a flex-test. Do you know what that is?"

Howard doesn't answer.

"It's simpler, cheaper, and you won't need anesthesia. And you won't have to go to Armstead." Armstead, a city fives time larger than Fletcher, is an hour south. "I can do it right here, in this room."

"Thanks for fixing my eye," Howard says.

She folds her arms the way football players do when they're watching the action from the sidelines.

At the desk, she staples his receipt to a stool sample kit. Exiting, he glances back from the door, and she winks. He'll start his next fire with the kit. The wink, he doesn't know what to do with that.

Ankles, his blue-heeler, recognizes his gait, ultrasonic hearing or something extrasensory, and rises from where she's lying on the seat of the pickup. When he gets in, she shivers and shows her teeth in a smiling grimace. He dodges her tongue, sets the kit on the seat around behind her. "Want your stool sampled?" he asks her. Still grinning, she tries to lick him again. On Rabbit Road, their dust is a long plume tilted to the south, burlap colored in a cold, sunless wind.

Carol Remmick phones two weeks later. "No blood, Howard," she says. "That's good. I can set you up Tuesday, Thursday, or Friday the week after next. Or those days any week after." She waits. "Howard?"

"Tuesday."

"I have another kit for you. Do you want me to mail it or do you want to come in and get it?"

"What kind of kit is that, Ms. Remmick?"

"Carol. A little something to clean you out for your exam."

"Oh boy, you know, on second thought—"

"If you don't come, I'll bill you as a no-show, and I'll lie to anybody who asks about it." She waits.

The night before the flex-text, Howard upcaps one of the plastic bottles in the latest kit and downs the contents. He curses, stretches out his tongue. The stuff is as heavy as water glass, a clear sodden density laced with a fake, cloying flavor. Shortly, he's posted in the bathroom. Later, in bed, his guts wrench, wring, and threaten total expurgation, even though there's nothing left to expel. He turns on the bed light. The windows are rattling. It's been blowing hard all night. The wind hasn't let up for five days. He opens Penn Warren's *All The King's Men* and ricochets from one sentence to the next, attends instead to the mutiny inside and to a mounting dread.

At dawn, he stands at the west window and watches the colors transmute across the giant cliffs of the reef. Gold, then orange to fuchsia, and finally mauve, then back again to orange. He goes back to the bedroom window and gazes east through the wind-frantic aspen toward town. Layered clouds over the Great

Plains are scarlet, raspberry below, purplish on overhead, most of it shredded by the crooked trunks, limbs, and twigs of the krumholz aspen, wind-bent trees tilted out as if sprinting for the horizon, fleeing for respite, any lee. The wind vibrates the copse in a sort of tetany so that through the tortured net of limbs and twigs a sky-dome of color pulverizes, fizzes, jitters like a million colored bubbles in an aquarium. Bits of snow jeer, fling back in gusting eddies, and click at the glass.

He lies on his back in the empty bathtub and stretches awkwardly to insert the applicator tip of the enema. Could the author of these instructions have imagined the ignominy, the unimaginable depletion this affair proscribed? Ankles is all perplexity when he latches the bathroom door on her, locks her out to save them both the shame.

In the time it takes to upend his crooked length into the cold cast-iron tub, he sees that original purposes have been compromised. This is an ordeal for mortifying flesh and spirit, for scarifying musty assumptions. House cleaning, big time. But is there any immunity, any resistance, he wonders, without dignity?

At the clinic, Nurse Remmick—Carol she demands again—tells him to have a seat, that it won't be long. Assuming that he hasn't eaten for eighteen hours, she can imagine he's impatient to get on, to have breakfast. Breakfast hasn't crossed his mind. His fret bucket is full with other matters. "I guess the only thing left I don't want to hear," he tells her, "is that you have to be in on this."

"I do, but it isn't like I haven't done it before, or that you're different from any other human being."

"Whether I'm the same or not, there are some places I'd like kept to myself."

"All I can say, Howard, is that I won't be taking any of this the way you think I will."

"How'd you like to switch places, Ms. Remmick?"

"What made you decide to go through with this, Howard? That's what I want to know."

"An exercise in self-improvement. Ultimate humiliation ought to be worth something."

She starts to say something, but doesn't.

"It's that arrangement of women and men. After getting his paint stripped, maybe a man wouldn't have to be smiling all the time, you know, like he's never scared."

"This has put you to thinking, Howard."

"Yes, it has. With no clothes on, there's no way to make it better than it is, but out there in the wind there's nothing wrong either. We didn't invent disgust. If we're a mistake, it's somebody else's mistake." He squints one eye.

She shakes her head. "You think too much."

"I've got nothing but time to think. What's your job in this nasty program?"

"I'll feed in the cable and retract it while Dr. Clement steers it." She hands him a gown with no backside.

"What's this supposed to cover?"

"So you don't get cold."

Melvin situates Howard lying on his side on the examination gurney, where he faces a blank wall. He tips his head back to glimpse the television monitor against the adjoining wall. Melvin is testing the projector end of the cable, a dark snake craning, kinking it's head about, looking back at the nurse and doctor, faces flying up in color on the monitor, their expressions bulbous and leering in the fish-eye lens.

"Why don't you stick that TV where I can watch, too?" Howard asks.

The ballooned faces on the monitor look at each other. "Why not?" Melvin says. She wheels it around to front Howard.

"You'll register some pressure from the air we feed in to expand the colon," Doctor Melvin says.

Howard feels what must be Vaseline smeared on. As with the impaled eye that started it all, he has to work at unclenching himself, but cooperation is irrelevant, for the cable penetrates by way of its own implacable authority. The intrusion is trenchant, violating, and Howard finds himself grinding his teeth. Courage, he summons. Besides, dignity is an illusion, nothing but putting somebody else's ideas into practice, somebody else's choreography. He shouldn't have to apologize for having an asshole. It wasn't his design that his exit had to be their entrance. Employees only.

A blurry, indistinct pink-lavender shows on the screen, and Howard is transfixed. Momentarily, he catches a cavelike opening, moist walls rumpled and twisting away into darkness, a little like looking down into an old high-top boot. The image blurs. When a little clarity shows, he feels the cable sliding, watches the field of view plunge ahead, again losing focus. "We're going all the way to the end right off," Melvin says. "When we get there, we'll back out slowly and give it a good looking over."

At once, Howard can follow the process of these two picking their way through his insides. The spelunkers search for an opening, then ease forward toward the darkness at the next fold. "So you two are old schoolmates," Melvin says, apropos of nothing. "You married, Howard?" The question, its odd context, seems a consequence of distraction. Or its aim.

"No," Howard says. "This snake with a camera has its own headlights and an air hose?"

"And a few teeth."

"Howard's been married. But he's divorced, twenty years ago," she says.

"Same as you," Howard says. "We both have grandkids in high school."

"Yes, we do. My grandson and his granddaughter are both on

the track team. About the only place I ever see Howard anymore is at those meets."

"Do you have a ranch, Howard?"

"No, I'm more like a mayordomo at the old Markle place."

"Howard works for David Strait," she volunteers. "Mends fence, don't you?"

"He's a good hurtler, that Willy, her grandson. And Karen's pretty good in the long jump and the triple jump."

"I see," the doctor says. "David Strait is your boss?"

"In a manner of speaking," Howard says. "Several levels removed." David Strait is a big name, the eastern tycoon who owns the largest ranches in the state. Howard has talked to him twice in his life, brief exchanges, both regarding Howard's opinion about the Tandy Ranch to the north, another spread Strait had his eyes on. His real boss, if that's the right term, is Strait's lawyer in Armstead. Howard doesn't care much for Strait. Or the lawyer. Both seem like they're playing poker, viewing any and every exchange as an obligation of supremacy, circling like wrestlers looking for a take-down, their universe being nothing but the pursuit of advantage. Neither has a clue how to pass the time of day. What leverage did either need over someone like Howard, who came with no poker chips to speak of, whose only table stakes were a few good stories and assorted memories?

The doctor wants to know what he does when the fence is all mended.

"I work on four miles of it a year. Of thirty-six miles on the ranch, it takes nine years to make a round. Then it's time to start over again. There are chores, too, daily stuff." He gets another shot of the wet, rosy cave. He couldn't be sure, but it looked like it was moving, his colon, the walls pressing in here and there, trembling. He tries again to encompass it, the monumental strangeness of it all.

"Didn't you ever want your own place?"

Howard considers to get the phrasing right. When Melvin murmurs something to Carol, Howard discards the question, and focuses again on the monitor. Melvin seems lost in a cul-de-sac of pink-purple drapes. "I think we're there," she says.

The camera backs away and takes in the rumpled gut. "Goddamn," Howard says.

"You all right?" Carol asks.

"Yeah," he says. "Tell me what're we looking for, what we don't want to see."

"Polyps," Melvin says, "little chunks that look like raw hamburger attached to the wall."

The camera backs down the channel. A small silvery disc shows on one surface. The camera stops. "What's that?" Howard asks. "Looks like a pitless adapter on a well casing."

"A slight abnormality," Melvin says, "nothing that matters. I don't think we need to take anything." The camera retreats. "Well..." Melvin equivocates, "won't hurt to get a piece. Since we're here." The view enlarges again. Startlingly, a chrome-colored lance appears at the bottom of the screen, a dart with a narrow pair of hinged jaws. Deftly, the dart stalks the disc, then plunges forward, impaling the disc, the jaws sweeping in, tearing a bit of flesh free. "Wo," Howard says.

"Did you feel it?" Carol asks.

"Like pulling a hair." Howard tries to reconstruct the sensation. The receding wall squirms, trickles a rivulet of blood. The silver lance, clasping its bit of flesh, withdraws from sight at the bottom of the screen. The camera tracks on down the colon.

"Here's a look at the back side of the moon," the doctor says. The image sweeps, dissolves, then coheres once more upon a constricted crater, petaled with radiating ridges, a black cylinder entering the side and penetrating the center. Howard realizes this is the end of the tunnel, a view of his sphincters from the inside. The cylinder is the cable, which like Howard, is presently viewing itself.

When the cable is retracted, and Howard is allowed to stand, the doctor hands him a wad of tissue for clean up. Carol is packaging the biopsy. "You're going to have some air escaping," the doctor says in a lowered voice.

"I guess if it's your air and not mine, I don't have to be embarrassed."

Carol shoots him a smile.

He marvels. "Maybe I've been enlightened? Now that the three of us have had our heads up my ass, I might never be embarrassed again."

"Good luck, Howard." She stands at the door with her hand on the knob. "You remember at that one track meet when it started snowing, and I offered you half my blanket? You'd have nothing of it."

"I was too shy," he says.

"Shy," she says. "Poo. And now you'd accept? Now that I've had my head up your ass?" The doctor waiting to exit behind her, glances back and forth at them.

Howard still has a wad of unused tissue in one hand and somebody else's fart knocking at his door. He's finding it hard to keep track of everything.

On the way home, he pulls off on the side road to Two Dog Reservoir and stops on the earthworks. Near the outlet in the blowing snow, a few ratty cottonwoods stripped of all color and respectability suffer what look like tremors of death. The pickup is buffeted; droplets spray the windshield. Ankles sits up, looks out, and then lies down again. There's something about the reservoir that can take any weather and magnify it past expectation, even when he stops here nearly every time to make the test. Whitecaps rip across. The water beneath looks hard and impenetrable as obsidian. A few coots cling to the tiny copse of shredded cattail in the nearest cove. Like a carnival ride when you're a kid, he's thinking, something you crank up as far as it will go, a thrill to feel it more, this goddamn earth. To feel it better.

# THE HAWK AT ARMAGEDDON

The day she met Maynard face-to-face, Tosh was witnessing with Lorna. Mostly, she watched Lorna witness. Maynard came to the door with reading glasses slid down to the end of his nose. His eyes, blue with dark flecks, studied them over the steel rims.

"We wanted to invite you to our church for a big service we're having in three weeks," Lorna said to him. She gave him the flyer. "It's an annual event where we have our best—"

"Jehovah's Witnesses?" he asked.

"Yes," Lorna said.

He nodded and then he looked at Tosh and pointed at her. "You're my neighbor. I've seen you riding your horse."

"Yep," she said. "And I've seen you with your hawk. And that big balloon."

He nodded. "You're welcome to come in, but I'm passed being saved. I'm a lost soul, so you're wasting your time."

"Nobody is a lost soul," Lorna said, which Maynard must have figured meant she wanted to come in. He stepped aside and, as they went into the room, they exchanged names.

"Tosh, that's an interesting one," he said.

"It's from Natasha. To keep folks from saying Naataaasha instead of Na-tawsh-a."

He scooted his glasses up a bit with the back of one hand and studied her, but it wasn't her name he seemed to be thinking about. He told them to sit at the table where he'd been working. Then, joining them, he picked up a square of leather and needle and thread. "I'm making a hood. This is to cover the falcon's head, so she won't get frightened or diverted by anything. It shuts off the lights for her."

"We want to bring the good message and the blessings of knowing Jesus Christ," Lorna says, almost as if reciting.

"I'm sorry. I've had Larry and Carolyn and who else…" He looked up and let his mouth hang as he mulled. "Can't remember who else. Joan, my wife, she won't listen, but I've talked to your people. I read some stuff about you folks. No eating blood, so no transfusions. I know about Armageddon, when God will send Satan away, and then the chosen get to live with God on the planet all cleaned up and made into heaven."

Lorna didn't say anything. It was as if she didn't have the notes for the way the talk had turned. The stitches didn't show on the little hat he was working on.

"It has a topknot," Tosh said.

"What?" Lorna started, then frowned.

"What he's sewing. That's pretty cute."

"This is what you grab for slipping it on or pulling it off," Maynard said and then he looked at Tosh up and down like her clothes or shape or whatever he was checking out wasn't any more off limits than her looking at the little leather helmet in his hands. She smiled at his interest. Rafe, her seventeen-year-old, had told her about Maynard's visit at the school with his bird. And now here she was in his house getting checked out. She turned a little to give him something from the side. She was aiming at forty, but she wasn't out of the picture yet.

"We have weekly bible meetings to discuss the scripture," Lorna told him. "If you had questions we could all help you with them."

"Right. Dogma, that's what I call it. Everybody's got their own scripture. And yours like most has all kinds of contradictions in it. You just cherry-pick the lines that back up what you already want to believe."

Tosh stared at Lorna to see what she was going to do with that.

"The teachings of Christ are pretty consistent," Lorna said.

Tosh was proud of Lorna for knowing that. She looked back at Maynard.

"You got any people in your church you'd call rich?" he asked.

"Some are better off than others," Lorna said. It sounded like she was looking for a tree to get behind.

"All these rich Republican Christians," Maynard muttered, "when your Bible, when Christ that is, says pushing a camel through the eye of a needle would be easier than getting a rich man into heaven. Those are the same folks searching the Bible from one end to the other to find something about spilling your seed on a rock."

"Excuse me," Lorna said.

"Oh that bit about playing with yourself, how spilling it in the valley of a whore is better. And the warnings about a man lying with a man, as if gay folks are some kind of enemy instead of somebody a little different from you and me."

"A lot of the Bible's teachings have to do with preserving the traditional family," Lorna told him. "People who believe it takes hard work to make good communities. And some of those other problems you mention have to do with the new law and old, with the two testaments."

"Oh, I know, I know. I don't need to get after you. It's just that you're here to change my mind from what I believe, and it just makes me want to change your mind about what you believe. You call it bringing the good message, and I call it thinking you know more about what I need to know than I do." And with that, he stopped stitching and looked hard at Tosh, like she was something on the pantry shelf he'd like to take off, open, and help himself to.

In the car, Lorna said, "We shouldn't give up on anyone, but I have the feeling we'd put our time to better use somewhere else." She was filling out their little form sheet.

"Right off, he warned us he was lost," Tosh said. "But he was pretty interesting, wasn't he?"

Lorna looked at her funny, those not-believing eyes going from round to squarish.

"What?" Tosh said.

Lorna's shrug was so small Tosh hardly saw it. Tosh shrugged, too. It wasn't her fault Maynard chose her to look at that way. If there was something wrong with liking the way he looked at her, she couldn't put her finger on it. Thou shalt not like being looked at?

"So he said you could ride on his place," Lorna said.

"Yeah, he did. And I'm going to do it."

"Did his staring make you uncomfortable."

"I didn't see him staring."

"Really?"

"Really."

\*

Cody works for his father, a building contractor. Tosh, Cody, and their son, Rafe, have two acres and trailer house. In the back, Cody built a miniature barn with several bunks of unplaned cull lumber and plywood blows, but all they have for stock are a bum calf and her horse, Bennie. An eight-year-old heeler named Ace and a flock of banties round out their living possessions.

Cody has always wanted to work for himself. He bought an old backhoe once, but it broke down every week and repairs cost more than the work he could find. He drove a logging truck for the Nelson brothers until they closed the mill. But Cody wants out from under his Dad's thumb. Even Cody's mother thinks that's a good idea. "Cody depends too much on what his father thinks," she told Tosh. "And Mel is Mel. He doesn't know anything else. He gets on Cody for being soft-hearted. Mel aims to raise Cody the way his Dad raised him."

That soft heart was one of the things Tosh loved about Cody, the way he'd try to wipe his eyes in secret in a sad movie or at Christmas concerts when Rafe was in grade school. He'd keep the sounds in, but she'd feel him jerk. When she'd look at him, his face would be all twisted and determined looking, but he was having a good cry inside. Cody was forty two, but it was like there was a little boy in him he couldn't keep boxed up. Sometimes she felt sorry for him. And sometimes she didn't, like whenever he called her dumb.

But he did all the man stuff. And cowboyed. He rode bucking horses at the Fourth of July rodeo and once he rode a bull. He got a deer every year and an elk twice and once even a bear. Big as he was, he was the one asked to help push a truck out of a snow bank, move a freezer or wood stove, or lift a ridge beam or a wall frame while others tacked it in place. But he wasn't tough enough to satisfy Mel.

A week ago, they banged heads. When Cody came home, he got his Bud Lite out of the fridge and went outside without saying anything. But instead of sitting in his lawn chair in the back yard, he leaned heavy on the fence, and Tosh could tell there was trouble. She popped a beer for herself and went out to stand alongside to see what was up or, in this case, down.

"Gotta get something going on my own," he said, not looking at her. "Got to. I can't work for that bastard anymore."

"What happened?"

"He's such an asshole."

"What happened?"

Cody didn't want to tell her, she supposed, because he didn't want go through it again. He shook his head twice slowly. "You know Liz Johnson lives across the road from where we're building?"

"Yeah?"

"Her border collie, she's a young dog maybe one or two years old, she came over where we were working, and I told her to go home. And I thought she did, but then she came back. You know, she wanted some company, somebody to play with. Well, I told her to go home again. This time I said git and slapped my hands. Off she went, ears down, tailed tucked under, up the roadbank, not looking, and here came Mel in his truck."

Tosh groaned.

"Whamp, that sound. You know like slamming the door on the chest freezer. Oh god." Cody turned his face away. "She was laid out flat in full gallop but nothing was moving. Gone, gone, gone."

"I'm sorry, Cody."

"I carried her over and laid her on Liz's lawn. Then I went to the door. Oh Jesus, Liz just went to pieces, broke down, oh God. It was so awful. Went on a long time," Cody's voice was thick and choked up. "Finally I asked her if I could bury the dog or dig the hole or something, but she just wanted me to go, so she could be alone with her."

"I'm sorry, Cody."

"Yeah, one of those things, aint it."

"Mel never came over?"

"Oh no, not Mel. He was busy. It wasn't his fault."

"What then? He said something because you tried to help Liz or felt bad for her?"

Cody made a sound like he was trying to get a bug out of his throat.

"He wasn't mad at you? I mean it wasn't your fault."

Cody turned his head away to wipe his eyes with the back of one fist.

"Oh," she said. "So I spose he said something. In front of the crew."

"I gotta get on my own."

"You don't have to be like him."

"I know that," he snarled.

"Sorrrryyy." She backed away.


So Cody knowing he had to be harder and meaner messed up other things that didn't need harder or meaner ways of thinking. A few nights ago at dinner, Rafe was telling them about the neighbors upset with Cody spraying his pasture; these were the people west of them, the parents of Rafe's friend, Paul.

"Goddamnit," Cody barked, "I didn't spray their pasture. I'm not letting knapweed take over like it has on their place."

"Paul says they're worried about it getting in the water."

"Water, what water?"

"The groundwater, I think."

"Oh Jesus, why don't they mind their own business? Billy Carlton's been using Milestone for years, and there's nothing wrong with him. I'd take a bath in it. What a bunch of goddamn whiners."

"Sometimes you sound just like your father," Tosh said.

"I sound like me." He spaced the words like he was getting sworn into duty.

Cody had that big heart all right, but he had to play the guy shoving on his helmet, loading his gun, going out to face the enemy, or zipping up his pants after having his way with a woman. Lately, she'd taken to having a light on when they made love. In the dark, it seemed he was more likely to imagine himself a buck or a bull, and he was rough and alone-seeming. With a little light on the program, he was more apt to take notice of her, to trace her parts with his fingertips and get wander-lost, his lower lip hanging idiot-struck, having forgotten about the supposed-to-be's of grunting and heaving and crushing her with his hairy, hoofed weight.

It was on her last birthday that Cody bought her the silver sea-bright banty-chickens: two roosters, the rest hens. Tosh had never seen chickens as pretty as these, feathers that were all white and black commas, scallops of India ink. Cody built a small coop out of loading pallets. They had the run of the yard and the weed-filled flower gardens Tosh started and then neglected around their trailer house.

When the one hen injured her leg somehow, she hopped about propping herself with her wings pushed down like crutches. Her breast got a little stained because she spent most of her time lying in the lawn grass. By and by, they could feed Lamey scratch from the hand. Soon after, Lamey would find them when they sat out in the lawn chairs. Hanging out, she lay beside them in the shade they cast.

When one of the other hens disappeared, Cody said he would build a fenced run. But he didn't get around to it for a few weeks, and then the missing hen showed up with six fuzzy, golf-ball chicks of her own. She'd have a fuss whenever anybody got too close, which often sent a rooster to attack. Sometimes when Tosh was filling the feeder or water pan, they'd fly at her and strike her legs with their wings and feet.

"You want me to fence up those little bastards?" Cody asked her. She was standing on a stool getting a casserole bowl down, and Cody was looking at the scratches on her calves.

"No."

"You like getting beat on?"

"I can deal with it."

"Yeah, you can." He slid his hand up her leg.

"Hey." She lurched away. Rafe was in the other room watching TV.

He tried again, and she smacked his head with her forearm, harder than she intended.

"Gees," he said. She could see his feelings were hurt. He went out the screen door.

She watched him go. "Oh boy," she murmured.

A few days after witnessing for Maynard, she rode Bennie down to the gate to his place. She had to get off the horse to open the wire fence into Maynard's and then do it again going back. She thought about lengthening the wire loop so she could do it mounted, but Maynard didn't seem the type who'd want any slack showing in his fence, no slump in the gate. She rode bareback and barefooted, bareback because they didn't own a saddle and barefoot because it made it all look wilder. When she was fifteen, she was on the front page of the Sunday paper. A photographer she'd never seen got a shot of her galloping through the pasture bareback and barefoot. Mindful of that image, she sometimes took to unbuttoning the top two buttons of her blouse.

She saw him out with the hawk her first day riding on his place, so she galloped through the cottonwood where he could see her flashing through the glades of light. When he gestured her over, she turned her back to him first, fastened one button on her blouse but left the other.

"Where's your balloon?" she asked riding up to him.

"I don't use it all that often. She's waiting for a quail today."

"Like she has a menu or something?"

"I'm her menu."

"So what's that balloon do?" She'd seen him flying it tethered like a kite.

"I put her food on it. Trains her to fly higher." With that, he slipped off her little cap and lifted his fist. Off she flew, her wings like flicking knives. "I tie a dead quail to it and put it up three hundred feet or so. She's got to go up there to get it. And that's good for exercise and training. I want her up high when she sees prey."

"I didn't know we had quail around here," she said.

"We don't. I raise them, chukars. I've got one cached over there." He pointed. "When she gets high enough, I'll release it with his little electronic doo-dad."

They watched the hawk circle higher and higher. The hawk was turning into a dot. "The higher she gets, the farther away she is from catching it," Tosh said.

"Yes, but she gets more speed in the stoop, her dive. And it's a helluva lot more spectacular."

They watched until he said, "All right. Hold your eye on the falcon."

She heard the quail fly, but she kept her head cranked back. The dot of hawk swerved and swelled in size. In a swiftly descending arc, it cometed down and then collided with the fleck of quail that came into view just above the horizon. Feathers burst out, one dot fell, the other shot straight up. The hawk circled once, twice above, then dropped down to where the other fell. Maynard started over. "What you think about that?" he crowed over his shoulder.

"That poor quail didn't have a chance."

"No," he conceded. "But this is just training. Soon as she's ready for wild birds, she won't be getting them all the time." He slowed to look at her. "You always ride bareback?"

"Got no saddle."

"A horse with no saddle?"

"Can't pay for both."

"I'd like to watch you get up on that animal."

"Oh yeah?"

"Yeah." He was looking at that undone button.

"Well, I use a bucket at home. At your gate, I got to hump my belly over. It's not too pretty. When I was girl, I could grab the mane, swing out, and high-jump it."

He turned away, murmuring something she couldn't make out. She was vaguely disappointed. It wasn't anything about the gate, she didn't think. He didn't seem as interested in her as he'd been the day she and Loren witnessed for him.

The hawk was on the ground tearing feathers out of the quail—beakfuls—and flipping them aside. Maynard scooped up the hawk and its prey. He had a small piece of meat on his glove and, when the hawk went for that, he slipped the quail away and hid it into a back pouch of his jacket. The falcon tore at the meat, the snapping sounds savage.

"What's that on his leg?" She pointed at the little cylinder with a wire sticking out.

"A radio transmitter. I've got a receiver with a directional antenna. So I can find her if she gets lost."

"I suppose he's even got a house of his own. Indoor plumbing and all."

"No plumbing, but she's got her own house, yes. A mews, that's what it's called."

"You ever had to use that radio?"

"Oh yeah. Sometimes she'll catch a bird on her own and feed up. I have to find her then, when she's got little need of me. A few times she spent the night out."

"But you knew you'd find her?"

"That's always a scary scenario, like waiting for a teenage daughter who doesn't come home."

"What could happen to her?"

"You never know. Owls take them. They're blind in the dark, sitting ducks for a hungry owl."

"Owls eat hawks?"

"Owls are fierce."

When the meat was gone, the bird remained in a crouch and swept its wet, black, and protruding eyes across the horizon as if to find what it had killed. Then it wiped its beak on the glove where it stood. It looked to Tosh like a creature that would eat its own young.

"What's his name?"

"Her. Shen."

"Shen? That's a pretty name."

"She's a pretty bird."

"Not if you're a quail."

The bird's feathers lifted out, made her twice as big, and then she shook. Then she compressed back down to her bullet shape. She didn't look like anything anybody else would want to eat.

"Isn't she beautiful?" Maynard asked, proud as any lover.

"As a shark," she said.

This seemed to baffle him, his brow wrinkling. He looked as the hawk maybe to see what she was seeing. Then he turned and looked at her, up and down as if she owed it to him, but then he got stuck at her foot and ankle. "What?" she said, lifting it out to see. "I step in some mud?"

He shook his head.

She pulled at her pant leg, slid it halfway up her calf, still pretending to look for mud. He stared on, then let his gaze follow up her leg and arm to shoulder and neck. "What?" she said.

But he didn't answer. He blinked finally, and that seemed to break the spell.

So it was a Saturday that was all-fall-down. The three of them were home, and it started with an argument in the kitchen. At the table, Rafe was stapling posters on lathe frames. He was helping with the campaign for county commissioner, but his candidate was a Democrat, also the challenger. "What's going on with you?" Cody wanted to know. He'd just come in from mowing and he was at the sink running water, waiting for it to get cold. He scowled at Rafe. Cody's great Uncle Harold had been a state legislator, a Republican, of course. Tosh was at the counter cutting celery sticks.

"It's what I believe," Rafe said. "The Republicans are only for themselves. And big money."

"Tell me one county issue where that's true," Cody demanded.

"Land planning," Rafe said.

"Oh, for Christ's sake, Rafe, nobody should be telling somebody else what they can't do with their land."

"You want this valley all chopped up like Goose Valley?" Rafe flung back. "All trailer courts and subdivisions?"

"You'll inherit this place, Rafe, and you want somebody saying you can't make a living with it?"

"I do."

"Oh, for Christ's sake, that's so easy to say when you don't have to make a living yet. All your rich liberals, they've got no idea what it is to be a working man."

"I agree with Rafe," Tosh said. "I wouldn't want to live here if it was like Goose Valley."

"Stay out of this, Tosh. You don't know anything about it."

"I do, too. I know I'd hate to live in Goose Valley."

"You don't know anything about land planning. Or zoning. You want people coming in saying you can't put that building in there, no extra bedroom here, no wrecking yards allowed. You can't raise chickens or pigs, or bring in any singlewides. And we don't want you sitting out there in your lawn chair without shirt and shoes."

"You're exaggerating," Rafe said.

"Yeah, you are," Tosh joined in.

"Jesus, Tosh, you don't know crap about politics."

"I do, too."

"All right, what's a liberal? What do they want?"

She jerked. "They want what Rafe wants." She looked at Rafe. He grimaced and seemed ashamed for her.

"Yeah, Tosh," Cody sneered. "If this were school, you'd have to copy off Rafe."

"I'm not stupid," she yelled at both of them and, kicking the door open, she lunged out. The banties scattered when she shot through the yard. She went down into the river bottom then swung over toward Maynard's. Walking fast, she dropped quickly down through the pasture of orchard grass, ducked down between the wires and crossed through the fence. When she heard a slow cadence of pounding—metal ringing—she turned toward the noise. Rounding a thicket of hawthorn, she saw Maynard hammering wedges into bolts of wood. He'd cut down a snag and had bucked it into sections with a chain saw. Equally spaced piles of orange chips made a big dotted line along the saw-shattered tree. His shirt hung on the up-thrust stub of a limb. Waist up, he was naked but for gloves, which he took off when he saw her approach. "Where's your horse?"

"I'm walking," she said. "Where's Shen?"

"Home." He gestured with his head. "But I'll be flying her soon as I quit here." The white hair on his chest seemed a little damp from sweat. He was looking at her all glittery like, as if he couldn't be happier to see her, his head tilted up a little, his eyes at work.

She smiled to see his interest so clean and undistracted.

"I didn't know you heated with wood," she said.

"I don't, not the house anyway. But I have a woodstove in my shop."

"Oh." She was looking at a finger-length scar below his collarbone.

"So," he said, "you got your shoes on today."

"I do."

"And your blouse buttoned."

"You can unbutton it, if you want."

"I would," he said and he stepped up to her and began unbuttoning. Everything was different.

When he cupped her breasts with his rough, warm hands, she undid his belt. Then it all went so very fast, her pants unbuttoned, one leg of her pants and her underpants pulled down and off, his pants and shorts hitched down to his thighs. It was like they were both afraid the other was going to stop it before it got too far. She was up on him in an instant, her arms around his neck, his hands cradling her thighs. Later, reviewing, the whole thing reminded her of the toy locomotive Rafe had as a toddler, wound up and flute-tooting across the floor, its whistle cap pumping up and down. Up and down she went with Maynard rooted upright there like a tree. How fast it went, and then the shuddering and idiot cries, the warm stillest clasping, just them panting with her wrapped around him like a snake. Then ever so slowly, he lifted her off him and lowered her to the ground. Back down to the ground, where she saw her shoe on its side and her empty, twisted pant leg.

They hurried again. Without talking, they put themselves back together. When that was done, they looked at each other, as if to see who they'd become.

"Wo," she said, "we got caught up."

"I'll say." He made an oval with his mouth and shook his head once. "In a hurricane." He was blinking a lot. "Of our own making."

"I wish we hadn't," she said, when it seemed to her he was proud of what they'd done.

"I don't. I don't regret a second of it."

"What about your wife? Your marriage?"

"What about it?"

"It doesn't seem very good now."

"It's all different now, isn't it?"

"This isn't a first time, is it?" she asked.

"Yes, it is."

"And you're that okay about it? I mean to go home and there you are with it?"

"It'll be different," he allowed.

"You'll tell her?"

"No."

"But you'll be different or something?"

"I don't know."

"You can just do this and then wait and see?"

"What are you going to do? You've got a husband and church, so you've got God to mess with, too."

"I know. I didn't think this would happen."

"You were aiming for it, I could tell," he insisted. "You could have yelled it in my ear, and I wouldn't have gotten the message any quicker, any better."

"So you wanted it, too, from the beginning?"

"I did. You're attractive, and you have a lot of spirit."

"That's the nicest way I could ever be called a slut."

"You're not a slut to me. Maybe I'm a cheater to you."

"You're a cheater to your wife, and I'm slut to my husband, even if he doesn't know it."

"Whatever you want to call us, I've no regrets."

"I don't think I better ride over here anymore."

"You know more about that than I do."

"So you'd be fine with me coming back. You...you..." she trailed off.

He nodded.

"Bad things could happen. Really bad things."

"Don't I know it?"


When she left Maynard, Tosh didn't want to go straight back home. In part she was afraid what had happened might show on her like a punched ticket. She went to the river, undressed from the waist down and washed herself and her underwear. She wrung the underwear many times not sure what to do with them. Finally, she dressed without them. She wandered about in the brushiest areas while twirling her underwear, first one direction, then the other. She recounted what it was she did that signaled Maynard to what he thought she wanted. And then there was the starting gun: one of them saying to go ahead and unbutton this blouse. Who was this woman hiding in the woods, swinging her underwear like a stripper? After an hour or so, when the underwear were reasonably dry, she put them on again and started home.


She was more than halfway across the pasture when she heard the shot. It came from their singlewide. She ran. Once in the yard, she couldn't see anybody. Still running, she circled the trailer. She stopped when she saw Cody on the front porch. "Cody?"

He pointed. "Goddamn hawk killed Lamey. So I shot it."

She saw the pile of jutting feathers. "Oh no, oh no, Cody." She held her hands up as if to clasp her face, but she didn't touch her skin. Half-circling, she approached the still feathers. "Oh God, Cody, that's Maynard's falcon, Shen. Oh god no. Is she dead?" Tosh put her hands over her eyes.

"Lamey?" he croaked behind her.

"No," she wailed, but she wouldn't look.

"They're both dead. Look. Nothing's moving. I have a right to protect my property. She was our pet."

"Oh god, Cody, you didn't have to shoot her. Couldn't you have scared her away?"

"He killed Lamey. He came in our yard and killed her. I get to protect my animals."

"But if Lamey was already dead...? And now they're both dead. You know how valuable that bird is? That's the bird Rafe saw at school at the assembly."

Cody started down the steps with the gun. Then he came back up, put the gun on the swing, and went down again. Tosh crouched at the birds.

The falcon, her wings half spread, lay covering Lamey. There was a spot of blood behind the falcon's eye. And she was so dead. It was as if any bird capable of all that much life had to be just as much all that dead, more dead than Lamey beneath could ever be. Cody slid the falcon off and flipped her over. "What's that?" He pointed at the small metal cylinder fastened to her leg by one of the leather straps. The antenna wire trailed down.

"It's a radio that tells Maynard where she's at. He's got a receiver that points the direction."

"So he's probably on his way?" Looking at her, Cody's squint seemed spooked. "I got my rights, Tosh. I didn't know it was his. But even if I did, I got to do something when—"

"You don't know, Cody, you don't know how valuable this bird is," she interrupted.

"I could guess, but how do you know that?"

"He lets me ride on his place, and I watched him training her."

"Jesus Christ, Tosh." He held out his hands as if they were offerings. "I'll tell him what happened. Anybody else would've done the same, just protecting what's theirs."

"All that complicated training and equipment and there she is, dead, for killing a chicken."

"For killing Lamey," he cries.

"I know," Tosh said. "Oh god, there he is." She could see his station wagon creeping along the county road. He passed from view when their lilac hedge eclipsed his car. Slowly, he went by as the two stood at the foot of the hedge looking at each other and listening to the crunch of gravel. "I got to go tell him," she said and started for the lane.

"I'm going to tell him just what I told you, Tosh," Cody called after her.

Tosh stood out on the road. Rafe wasn't around, and she was glad of that. She knew Maynard would turn around soon, when the radio signal dimmed. Ten minutes later, she could see his car returning. Her eyes welled, and she choked a little. Furiously, she scratched her forehead. She heard him accelerate. She was standing in the middle of the road rubbing her face and looked up finally when she heard his door open.

"Oh no," he said. "Oh no."

"He didn't know," she gurgled. "Cody didn't know she was yours. She killed Lamey, our chicken, and he…"

"Is she…?"

"Yes. I'm so sorry, Maynard."

He went round her. She ran to catch up. She heard Cody say that the hawk had killed their chicken. "I was just protecting our pet," he said.

Maynard went down on his knees. "Oh no. Oh God no," he said wetly and lifted her up so very gently, her head and tail swinging a little. Tosh saw he was crying softly.

He stood slowly, met Cody's gaze, and started to say something but stopped. "What would you do, man?" Cody asked him.

"Leave him be, Cody," she said.

"I don't shoot first," Maynard croaked, "and then look."

"Listen, I'm sorry, but I did look, and what I saw was this hawk killing my chicken."

"I would've bought you a hundred chickens."

"But she was a pet. You don't buy a pet."

"You didn't have to kill her," Maynard whispered. All the spirit and air seemed let out of him. Leaving, he looked crumpled, bent over his dead bird. He went around the hedge and up the lane to his car.

"Oh man," Cody said.

They didn't hear from Maynard. One of Cody's buddies said that he could've pressed charges because that particular falcon was a protected species. "That isn't right, is it?" Cody asked Tosh. "That he can buy a protected species to kill our pets?"

Tosh didn't answer. She didn't have an answer. She quit riding on Maynard's place, but going and coming she rode along his fence, so that if he ever saw her, he could call to her. She'd already decided she'd not cross that fence no matter what. But she didn't see him down there, and it puzzled her. If he took it all as a punishment for what they'd done, who did he think was in charge? If he didn't believe in God, that is. If he was the lost soul he said he was.

For her own part, she didn't know what exactly she wanted as any kind of outcome. Eventually, she decided what she wanted most was to see him somewhere else, in town maybe. He'd want to have coffee with her, yes, that would do. And it would go no further. They'd drink coffee and talk about the county commissioner race or something like that.

# ASLEEP IN A STURGEON

*Five thousand times around the sun, and here I am back in the company of men. Sixty-two thousand moons, and I haven't forgotten the touch of the human hand. Am I shivering?*

*If my spirit got snagged in ice with a long-time body, if I never got cut loose, left to silt back into some sea of rest and dispersion, I still haven't had any explaining or reason for having been marooned like this. Why am I the witness?*

She was at the edge of the glacier near a fringe of rocks, halfway out, a shriveled body, the color of old brick, face down, part of her head and her back and butt showing and the backs of her thighs. But they didn't know she was a she then. In fact, it took some inspection to make out that she was human and not some departed alien. Her ribs, her backbone and hip, poked up, lifting her skin like a ridge or tent poles. The corpse was stiff as latigo leather but not entirely frozen. "This guy's been here awhile," Ernie said. He'd seen her first.

"It's against the law to mess with a body, aint it?" Johnny asked.

"How'd we know it was a body?" Ernie returned. "He could've been mostly buried, and it wasn't till we dug enough that we could see what he was." Ernie was on his knees scraping snow. "Let's get him loose. He's shrunk up like a pecker in a blizzard. I'll bet he's been here ten, twenty years."

They were at the head of Little Money Creek in a lift of glaciated mountains so steep and sudden that the two men could stand on the nearby divide and make out a line of moving specks on Highway 43. It was September, and they were casing out a hunt where, earlier on summer fishing expeditions, Ernie had sighted several big bucks. It was still a month before deer season when they spied the backside of the icewoman on Locust Glacier. She looked like she was snorkeling, as if searching the deep for pockets of the locusts also imprisoned there, namesake hoppers swept up in a prehistoric storm.

*I am the old-time woman who knows too little and too much. Stranded in this exile of ice, made to listen, I must know more than anyone else about my animal clan of naked-skin, hind-leg walkers. Not even the Maker knows as much as I do, because not even the Maker could stand to listen to them for as long as I have, their voices filtering up from all the valleys. If I've been chosen for special punishment, it's not because I am any sillier, any more contriving, or wickeder than any of the two hundred fifty generations I've followed.*

"What I want to know," Ernie went on, chipping with his knife, "is what kind of clothes these are. They're friggin' shot." Like wet cardboard, pieces stripped off with chunks of snow. "Same with his hair. Where's the rest of his hair?"

Johnny knelt and scratched at the thin glassy shell around the head. "It's there, his hair, but it breaks in pieces with the ice." He sits back on his heels. "How come he doesn't stink? Even though he's half thawed?"

"He's freeze dried. The guy's a chunk of jerky." Retrieving a clod of snow with a square of clothing embedded, Ernie turned it to the light, pulled off a glove, and scratched at it with his thumb nail. "Naugahyde," he said, "This guy was wearing Naugahyde. No wonder he froze to death." He touched the body, traced the bumps of backbone. "Come on. If we dig enough on this side, we can roll him over."

*At the start, I mostly listened to the voices of girls, followed them through their adolescence and marriage, through their loves and thefts, the rearing of their children and grandchildren, and then their decline. I heard their last words and the sound of their spirits leaving, like the wing sounds of the raven passing overhead. At first I missed them with the ache of living. With time, I learned to keep my distance. In that distance, I heard the voices of other valleys and came to know of other people. Their clothing and food differed and their gods and heroes and songs were not the same, but underneath, their stories resembled ours, in telling about what scared and killed them, what bound their clans, what made them thrive.*

*Stranded as I was, accumulating these impressions, I began taking up with men as much as women, following their lives, and in this I made another discovery. When men were most unlike women, what they intended—all the fighting and competing—they did it for the women. I saw how men and women shaped each other, women chosen by men for keeping good the agreements and community, while women chose men for a simpler, convenient loyalty fit in among the sweat-smelling bouts of building and defending. Or attacking. From there, all the misses and messes that followed between the sexes got passed off to what they couldn't understand about each other. But it wasn't sex that mattered most. If anyone says sex is a powerful force, tell them there's more power in what the neighbors have to say. About anything.*

*Of course, there were all the events and catastrophes I could not turn from. Battles, landslides, killer storms, and all the dramas of the family and clan. What surprised me was how many of these struggles* of failure and triumph occurred in the same places. There's plenty of ground that has no attraction whatsoever for the human imagination, whereas other sites drew people as dogs to scent. Of these plots, some seem fated by the blood of those spilt before. In this valley, for instance, a hundred generations ago, two brothers fought for the leg of their dead sister on the little rise above the fork of what they're now calling Elbow and Morley Creeks. In the end all three starved, their voices snuffed out like candle flames in the February wind. In another era of famine, a grandmother died in that same place. She'd been slipping her portion of food (a mouse, two minnows found frozen in ice, a stripped underpart of cottonwood bark) under the robe of her grandson. Only three generations ago, again on the same knoll, a rancher hanged himself from the barn rafters after learning that his wife and daughter, who had traveled east, swore to never return. Last year, a landowner shot his tenant's dog on that same plot after the dog killed a goose. Burying the dog, hiding its body, his shovel struck a mineralized chunk of hipbone from the starved brother. Sometimes I can hear the voices of the dead layered under those of the living, the dead brother still murmuring a prayer song, still crying for his sister's forgiveness. The ground is marked by these voices, by the blood of a goose and a dog as well. Sand and clay, bits of ash and rust and bone, mingled with sobs and laughter and chants, the shrieking gander. Dirt is a requiem.

They chopped with their knives, accumulating a berm of corn snow, which they pushed away with the sides of their boots. Then they dug around the body's feet and head and then on the other side around an outstretched arm, until they could roll the corpse. When it flopped over, the body carried with it a keel of crusted corn snow.

"Oh Jesus, we broke off a finger." Johnny examined the hand of the flung-out arm.

"We can chip it out."

"How'd he get here, Ernie? What was he doing? No skis, no gun."

"Maybe he fell out of a plane."

Tapping ice clinging to the emaciated body, they broke away fragments. "I'll bet he don't weigh but sixty pounds," Johnny said, testing the weight of a leg. The body was so shrunken that the knee was bulbous, the thigh finned with collapsed muscle, the pelvis with winglike hips rimming a hollow bowl.

"I think he lost his noogies."

"Yeah, or sucked 'em up inside when he froze."

"You spose the sheriff has any record of somebody missing up here?"

"He won't want us messing with the body," Johnny said.

"Like it's a crime scene, you mean?"

"Sure, instead of feeding the fishes, they left him to the eagles."

"I don't think so. He froze to death on account of wearing upholstery. What's this?" Ernie fumbled at something caught in the four-fingered hand. When he chiseled at the hand with his ax, a pale object broke away and rolled into the loose snow. Ernie sifted it out, righted it, held it up on the flat of his hand. It was a thumb-sized figurine of an animal, crudely carved. He tapped it with his ax and it rang like stone. A mountain sheep maybe, lying down, a curl of horn pressed up against each side of its face. Ernie whistled.

"This guy's somebody else, Ernie. Somebody olden."

"Really olden maybe, like those mammoths they found in the icebergs." He touched the corpse's hoisted arm. "This here is a discovery, Johnny."

"You mean like scientific?"

"Don't you think?"

"Like a man? Pillsbury Man, somebody like that?"

Ernie's eyes went fuzzy with imagined acclaim. "We ought to get something for this."

"Maybe."

*Stopped in ice as I have been has given me time to despair, to won-*
*der why the quick, the living, never catch on, why the wretched work*
*themselves to death for their children, so that their children can do the*
*same for the next generation. Where does this go? There's only one long*
*lyric sung from one generation to the next. I know every phrase by heart.*
*That's the attraction for an idea like reincarnation, you see. Eternal life,*
*yearn for it, but you could stand it only if you got to forget it all. After*
*the first thousand moons of a remembered life, I needed it erased. But*
*here I am, thousands of moons later, the unwilling watcher.*

*Sometimes I try for solace in the voices of younger people, in earshot*
*of minds not yet halter broken. A five-year-old girl amuses herself—and*
*me—with images for the names of friends and family: William's name*
*is like a bending pole; Larry is long and orange with an oval hole in the*
*side, while Philippa is in her underwear: Jill has a long neck; and Polly*
*two heads back to back like bonnets that are purple and smooth; and*
*Kaki with her face turned to the side has dots along her nose. Once,*
*hearing a cello, she thought it sounded like vanilla smelled.*

"You know what? I think we can get this guy down the mountain. You take my day-pack. If I carry him like a plank over one
shoulder, I just lean over and stand him up when I need to rest."

"What about if we aren't sposed to mess with bodies?"

"Look, this guy's been forgot for a million years. This guy's
back from the stone age, and he's not missing. He's worth something, I can tell you that. Somebody will want him bad."

"How bad?"

"My cousin east of the mountains has a neighbor who got a
new tractor after selling a dinosaur skull."

"This is a guy, Ernie. A somebody."

"He's no taxpayer. No voter. This guy should be dust, but he aint. We found him. He's ours. He's too old to belong to any government. I'll bet we can sell him."

"You don't know that."

"There wasn't any law for Garret's neighbor selling that skull." Ernie cradled the body at the hips, hefted it experimentally, and replaced it. "I'll be done in when I get to the bottom, but I think I can do it."

Ernie got three hundred yards before his first rest. He carried the corpse face down with the abdomen on his shoulder, his arm hooked around the body's waist. Johnny helped him lower the body onto its feet. Ernie held him up one handed, the way a crossing guard might hold a stop sign. Johnny had the stone sheep and the broken-off finger in his daypack, in his zip-lock sandwich bag.

"I'm thinking," Ernie said, wiping at his forehead, "that maybe we could get an auction going."

"Auction off a body?"

"Why not?"

"If he's older than the hills and they want him, they'll just find some law where they can take him away from us."

"They don't even know about this guy. He's with us, and we got to look out for him."

"They might condemn him, like they did Marston Flats for the new highway."

"They do that sometimes." Ernie agreed without enthusiasm, inspecting the slight, almost skeletal figure alongside. A dark mass of frozen clothing still stuck to the front of the torso like an applique. The sunken eyes were enormous, tangerine-sized cavities, the lips pulled back baring gumless long teeth, the nose more like a flattened tent than a central prominence. The arm still crooked before the face, seemed to be warding off a blow. "What's your name?" Ernie asked, then folded at his waist and hoisted his load back upon his shoulder, the corpse's arm shuddering with the movement but held now as if to shield away the sight of his descent. The holes in snow left by Ernie's boots followed the fall line. For however long this guy had been on the mountain, Johnny was thinking, here he was, heading back down to the same valley he'd left a long goddamn time ago. Haltingly, crookedly, they made their way off the lower end of the glacier and onto the landslide of black, angular rock. "I'm just saying," Ernie wheezed, "nobody even knows but us who's got him. We ought to get expenses, for Christ's sake."

Johnny said nothing.

"We could of been digging for a month, you know. If he was deep in."

Johnny remained silent.

"This is a discovery, I'm telling you. What you got against a bunch of money?"

"Nothing, if we can get it."

"Remember 'The Devil's Ransom'?"

"The movie?"

"Yeah, doing it like that, using newspaper ads for messages. And cell phones for drop-offs. At night."

"You mean, like he's a hostage? When they don't even know what we got?"

"The finger, Johnny. We give them the guy's finger."

Johnny smiled, then sobered. "There's no way we won't be breaking some law. Besides, how sure are we this guy isn't somebody's grandpop? Walked away from the nursing home in his rendezvous outfit?"

"Worst case, we leave him on Garret's lawn." Lloyd Garret had the only funeral home in Fletcher.

The rocks made for slow going. In an hour, they reached the timber and then took another half hour to maneuver a short stretch of downfall before they got to the trail. Ernie leaned his load against a tree, scraped at his shoulder where some of the clothing or skin had stripped off. "How much room you got in your freezer?"

"Not enough."

"Mine neither. But how about if we fill mine with some of your stuff. Will he fit then?"

"Let's fill mine with your stuff and put him in yours. What do I tell Lulu when she finds a body in the freezer?" Lulu, Johnny's daughter, was staying with her father until she got a job. Or run off with Callan, the guy she was seeing.

"Who's most likely to be nosing around in the freezer. My Marlyss or your Lulu?" Marlyss was Ernie's wife.

"You're not going to tell Marlyss?"

"We don't tell nobody till it's done. We keep all our options. For jumping ship or whatever. Can you lock your freezer?"

"Hell no. A locked freezer. The first thing that says is what the hell's he hiding in there?"

*After children, I sometimes visit the aged, envy those standing at the edge. And pity them. Even in my jealousy for their looming destiny in flames or moldering earth, I am angry for them, too, for their treatment, their loves lost, senses eroded, memories and minds stolen, dignity forgotten. Most are denied enough wherwithal to manage their own exit. After a life of dreading death's horror, they often go on hanging around, long codas marinated in raw pain (for what purpose, whose?), before they are culled finally, and there's nothing pretty about that either.*

*If I haven't been able to arrange my own disappearance, I would, at this moment, love to anticipate my imminent change of address, but this sounds ridiculous. Out of the glacier and into the freezer. And besides that, I already miss my finger. Even as I yearn for disintegration, I don't want to do it piecemeal. Or lose what's still keen in me. Nor do I want to be exclaimed over or marveled upon, when all I represent is a lot of*

*time. Old meat who can't cover her ears. I'd rather be grist for ants,*
*asleep in a sturgeon.*

*Come boys, build a fire. Throw me in, toss my finger after, and let*
*me go home.*

Lulu Carter kept a quart each of chocolate-chip-mint ice
cream and raspberry sorbet in the freezer compartment of the refrigerator. Every night she put a scoop and a half of each in a bowl
along with two ginger snaps, sat on the couch with the TV off, so
as not to dilute her focus, and worked her way through dessert in
tiny quarter-teaspoon bites.

When Johnny raided the mint-chocolate, and she found only
a few tablespoons left, tamped like green putty in the carton's corners, she went to the freezer on the back porch for a reserve quart.
But she found the chest lid stacked with trunks of her childhood
books, bundles of surveyor's stakes, drawers of pipe fittings and
electrical parts, coils of wire, three deep-cycle batteries from the
boat, and other cartons of who-knows-what heaped to the ceiling.

"Dad," she bellowed, careening through the house, but Johnny was not there. Were they conspiring? Her father and her boyfriend, were they planning to slim a few pounds off Lulu? Callan
called her his Clydesdale, but it wasn't altogether affectionate. She
yanked a box of tiles off the top and, surprised by their weight,
staggered, wobbled, lowering them to the floor. Mightily, she
kicked the box. It wasn't until after clearing the freezer lid she
realized she probably wasn't the target. Not if they left the sorbet
behind, which they had.

Whatever it was Johnny had stretched out in the freezer came
wrapped in a canvas tarp, a frozen bundle stiff as sheet metal.
Game? A half a deer? She lifted one end up. A king salmon? Sorting beneath, she retrieved the ice cream. Leaving the mess of cartons and junk on the porch floor, she took her dessert bowl to the

front steps and waited for her father. Distracted, she found herself unable to keep from taking large spoonfuls.

Johnny came in the back door. She heard him cry out. "Oh Jesus," he wailed. He had the chest door up when she arrived. "For ice cream?" he yelled. "You'd move all that for ice cream?"

"What's this all about, Dad?"

"They got no right coming after us." He was leaning on the lifted door.

"What?"

"We turn her over, and they're famous for nothing they did. We don't, and it's federal charges."

"Her? Jesus Christ, Dad."

Ernie was on the phone. "This is an emergency, Lulu."

"He's not here. Why'd you get Johnny into this, Ernie?" She could hear the seashell hollow on the other end, the sound of dread maybe. Or revising. "Look, Ernie, I know about her. You guys are idiots. I know you talked Johnny into this."

"When did he tell you?" Ernie's voice went soft.

"You can't pull this off, Ernie."

"Look Lulu, there's no time for chatting. I can't wait for Johnny. They're saying they've got leads, in the paper this morning, but that's bullshit, I know it is. Still, we got to get her out of your freezer now. Move her."

"I'd like that."

"You gotta help me."

"Over my dead body, Ernie."

"You got to do it for Johnny. They won't let me away from here till noon. I'll meet you past Barrett's Nursery, that first lane down to the river. The old Lover's Lane."

"I'm not doing it. I won't lug around a body. Besides, I don't have a car."

"Where's your car?"

"Callan's got it. I'm waxing his truck today."

"Truck's better.

"I can't drive it."

"What?"

"He won't let me. Not after that diesel thing." Lulu had confused the hoses at the pump several weeks before and filled one of the tanks with diesel fuel. She realized the mistake before starting up. But she had to call Callan and deal with his tantrum while they got it pumped out.

"Listen, Lulu, I'll sit on Callan if he needs sitting on. The guy in the tarp, there's nothing to him. He don't weigh more than a case of beer. You can drag him easy. It's your Dad's ass, too, you know."

"Her, Ernie. She's a her. You got him into this, didn't you, Ernie? This wasn't Johnny's idea, was it?"

"It's a partner deal, all the way. Look Lulu, I can't argue with you. The soonest I can get away from here and meet you is by one. Just meet me by the river, and I'll take him from there."

"I'm not—" She stopped when she heard Ernie speak to someone in the room with him.

"Gotta go," he came back. "Don't let Johnny down, Lulu." He hung up.

Lulu lurched at the click. She held the phone at arm's length and swore at it.

At the river, Lulu broke, bent, and tied off willows along the road's edge to keep them from scratching the truck. In the bed, streaks of frost edged the folds of canvas around the body. Hearing a diesel engine start up in the distance, she leaped into Callan's truck and pulled it farther into the obscuring thicket. A logging truck passed on the county road. She got out and went back to breaking willows. At length, satisfied nothing would scrape Callan's beloved ox- blood-burgundy paint job, she drove through the willows and into a clearing, and there backed the truck around on a slope above the river's edge. She set the emergency brake and got out.

Across the river, a heron made all its magical extensions and lifted away like a flying carpet. Blue gray and undulant as the water. Behind, the slender lines of willow and knobby charcoal of cottonwoods merged into the jade fir. Downstream, the heron crossed in front of a ridge of stone and a cliff overhang, where black water stains on the tan rock above resembled a face. Lulu, gazing at the flame-shaped stains, made out the visage of an old woman, cleft skin, dewlapped, hard squinting eyes, penetrating and severe, enraged or maybe laughing. It was hard to say.

Lulu inhaled powerfully, intending something, anything. She turned and went to the rear of the truck where she inspected the trussed lump of frozen, ancient woman, formless in this box of angled chrome and enameled steel. Callan had steel carrier-cases bolted everywhere, rimming the bed of the truck and on the running boards, the same burgundy and chrome loaded with enough parts and tools to build another truck. In one, he'd housed an extra battery wired on an alternate circuit to the generator. Clamped in other boxes, he had fire extinguishers, an army shovel and pick, tow straps, extra water and gas tanks, flashers and flares, tire chains, a mechanical and hydraulic jack. He had the cab provisioned with a fuzzbuster, a CB radio, and other unknown electronics, plus assorted tarps and blankets and ropes and bags. Anything anyone would ever need, provided they could find it.

A month before, when she and Callan had a flat tire, the only thing he lacked was the strength and size to break the lug nuts loose. "Goddamn them and their goddamn air wrenches," he wailed. She took the star wrench from him, jumped up and down a couple of times on it, and snapped it loose. He took the wrench back and tried another, trampolining this time, but Callan, all of five-foot-six of him, didn't have the gravity. She was afraid he might break a vessel in his head. "Got no lead in your butt," she told him and loosened the rest. He'd sprained his wrist with one enraged effort, so that for two weeks he couldn't pick up or handle anything without stifling a yelp. He didn't want her to tell anyone about it. "Call me Captain, when you need to rotate your tires," she said. Callan was a captain in the National Guard. He had an unhealthy respect for respect.

When Ernie arrived in his clunker Suburban, she was standing on the bank watching the river. He pulled up alongside Callan's truck. He laughed, relieved apparently. "Hey Lulu, I got it all figured out now."

She didn't say anything.

"Thanks to you," he tried. He walked around to her, and they watched the water.

"How the hell were you going to pull off a ransom, Ernie? How were you going to do that?"

"Everything went like it was sposed to, except when they got so excited and got the feds in and then the Indians, for Christ's sake, that Repatriot thing."

"How'd they know anything if they haven't even seen her?"

"We sent a finger."

"Jesus, Ernie," she said, a lip curling. "You sound like the Mafia."

"It was already broke off. We didn't mean to do it. But they gave us a phone number to an answering machine. So we could tell them what to do. Without getting into any back-and-forth shit. Our idea. My idea."

She squinted one eye.

"I'm no idiot. We had them post the number in the personal

ads. Under the woman who wanted to find the guy who left his gloves during his driver's test."

"You watch too much TV, Ernie. How were you going to get the money without getting nailed?"

He examined her as if she were going to turn into an undercover cop.

"Ernie, I brought her here, for Christ's sake. Quit acting like I shouldn't know everything."

Looking out over the water, he spoke in a lowered voice. "The viaduct over the railroad tracks north of Fletcher. You know, past Beaver Creek. We tell their delivery boy to get in and drive, giving him directions over a cell phone while he's driving, so then we tell him to stop on the bridge and toss the packet over the edge down on the tracks. Then he turns around and heads back. One car, one guy. No funny stuff. We snag the packet. There's a trail, a half mile to the old highway out to Wind Flat. They can't get out to that highway for eleven miles. By then we've gotten to Wind Flats, stashed the money there, and then back out to the main highway where we're the same as anybody else. Next day we tell their answering machine where we've left the body."

"Goddamnit, Ernie."

"What?"

"You're still gonna do it."

"Why not? First, I'm going to stash him where nobody can find him. Nobody but me. They want him. We want them to have him. We've saved them plenty. A finder's fee, you know. And delivered, too. Two more days and it's done. That's all. They get the fossil. We get expenses."

"Her, Ernie, not him. And Johnny's not in on it."

"The hell—"

They heard a click. Both turned. Callan's truck was rolling backwards toward the cutbank, and the river below. Ernie grunted

189

and ran, Lulu following. Behind his van, they stopped to watch the rear of the pickup drop over the knee-high cut bank. In the water, the rear part of the bed and tailgate listed toward the downstream side and then submerged. High-centered on the cutbank, the truck ceased moving and held fast. It looked like it had just shot up out of the core of earth, and skybound, froze for a moment at the edge of the river. The tarp-wrapped body buoyed up and over the tailgate, eddied out into the current and swept into the deeper, greener water. Ernie barreled into the river, charging with a drag-retarded lope, waist deep. Going deeper, he slanted out and stroked off after the gyrating, rolling tarp. Lulu ran along the shore. Across on the cliff, the water-stained face pattern watched on. When Ernie reached the body, he struggled to encompass it, tightening the unfolding slabs of canvas. Bobbing in the rapids, his head went under twice before he managed to roll his shoulder out and sidestroke, the load clamped under his other arm. His gulping and coughing jerked with urgency, but he wouldn't let go of the tarp, its buckled folds lifting like paddles then slipping again back under.

Ernie found footing near the middle of the river, stood in the current, bent, still coughing, lost in exhaustion, clutching like a child with a blanket. He pulled and gathered, but it was clear then to both that the tarp was all he had. Wilting a little, he let go of it, watched it slide away, and then he staggered toward Lulu and the shallows.

She met Ernie in the water, took his arm, waded to shore with him. "I had it set, Ernie. You know I did. You'll back me up."

"What?" His eyes protruded.

"You heard it pop out, Ernie, the emergency brake. I know you heard it."

It was the ford at Old Woman Rock, where the face showing

in stained rock looked out over the high water. The sun was near its zenith, but clouds were stacking up. Soon, days of rain would give over to summer, to dry heat that would turn the cherries red and eventually black. But on this day, the river thrashed, slick brown roils flinging by trees with roots stuck out like lightning.

They'd been digging camas, she and her daughter, in the blue-flowered meadows across the river. They'd forded where the herons had their colony on the island. With a pole in one hand, and her little girl under her arm, she waded the first channel in waist-deep water then crossed beneath the swarm of nests spread high in the cottonwood canopy. Great croaking blots wheeling overhead, the huge birds spewed out above. The smell of ordure was fishy and bitter. Gazing upward, she shivered when she saw the skeleton, wings spread, white leering bones spread in the net of limbs. A bone-beaded neck arched like an angry rattlesnake, the hollow orbits of missing eyes glared down over the perfectly tapered blade of its beak. Snatching the girl up under her arm, she ran again. The current in the second channel was as strong as in the first, and she had to return, break down a cherry sapling and strip the limbs for another staff.

They had almost a full bag of bulbs when the rain came. She threw down her digging stick and surveyed the river, first upstream then down, and returned to the ford below. The water was deeper there than above, but she didn't want to go back under the skeleton leering over the lip of nest. The rain fell harder, stippling the swollen, twisting belly of river. Hesitating seemed a deadlier approach, so she charged in. But midway, she saw what was coming, what she could not stop. She let the camas go, then the pole. The force of water sprayed gravel out from under her feet. A heavy silence enveloped them, twisted her softly, and gently crushed her chest, the surrendering easy at first, soft as the journey of clouds, the two of them rolling together, until the tearing pulled the girl from her. Far downstream, the robbed woman crept from the water onto a mud bar.

But the loss, that, too, was not dependable, not even death. Worse was the death of death. In every season thereafter of blue camas and high water, of nesting herons, the picture fragments of her daughter eroded. A bumblebee cupped, clasped buzzing within those two chubby and fearless hands, a bumblebee that did not sting her. A good memory like that one withered with too much use. There was the one of the toddler dragging the burning ends of willow and cottonwood limbs to the creek where she thrust them in and made them hiss and bubble. It was her giggling that made everyone laugh. This stopped daughter, she got all used up.

In the moon of first frost, the mother left alone for the mountains, climbed to the headwaters of the creek above where they camped. She ascended the rock, then the ice. She brought with her the stone amulet of the bighorn along with a new kind of memory, a made-up one. They climbed together until dark and then, glassy with sweat, crossed the glacier in moonlight. In this vision, her daughter was older, a young woman so tall and fine. They sat at the edge of the ice and talked. Clouds streamed in and snuffed out the moon, and snow began falling, heaped around them deep and light. It seemed better there than in the valley, so they never went back down.

# ACKNOWLEDGMENTS

Thank you to Tim Schaffner and all the journal editors who helped refine these stories, and most of all to Janet McGahan, whose good eye and good sense made every story better.

# AUTHOR BIO

Jerry McGahan is a writer, a painter, and a photographer. He is the author of *A Condor Brings the Sun* and his short fiction has appeared in numerous literary journals, including *Antioch Review, Georgia Review, Gray's Sporting Journal,* and *Ploughshares*. His work has appeared in *American Bee Journal, the Journal of Experimental Biology,* and *National Geographic*. He lives in Arlee, Montana.